I0684424

Nice

———

A Novel

Karin Gustafson

BackStroke Books

This is a work of fiction. Any resemblance to actual persons or events, with the exception of historical or public ones, is purely coincidental.

Copyright © 2014 NICE by Karin P.E. Gustafson
Copyright © 2014 NICE cover image, and interior image by Karin P.E. Gustafson
Published by BackStroke Books
All rights reserved , including the right to reproduce this book or portions thereof in any form.

Parts of this book have appeared in slightly altered form on
http://Manicddaily.wordpress.com.

ISBN 10: 0981992358
ISBN 13: 9780981992358
Library of Congress Control Number: 2014909359
LCCN Imprint Name: Arkville, New York

Also by Karin Gustafson
1 Mississippi
Going on Somewhere
Nose Dive

For my beloved parents.

NICE

Les
Suburban Maryland
June 1968

Her big brother Arne was first to find it.
They didn't usually talk much. He was fifteen, she not yet eleven.
But one afternoon after school he called out to her. "Hey, dopey, you
want to see something?"

He opened a drawer in her mother's bureau, one of the new maple
ones, and stared down into it.

Just below a jumble of purses–brocade for spring, black patent
leather for winter, lay a turquoise gauze negligee with turquoise feathers
around the neck. A black bra cuddled inside the negligee and, next to it,
a basket of white rubber ring things wrapped in clear plastic.

She would not have believed the negligee and bra without seeing
them herself. The white rubber things sent a chill down her spine. From
Arne's glare, she knew that they too must have something to do with sex.

But her parents slept in twin beds, slim little beds with white-fringed
bedspreads, beds that weren't even side by side but foot to foot.

Her parents loved each other, sure. But her dad made a big deal
about just giving her mom a kiss and even then it was always on the
cheek.

Her mom had small dark eyes, a sharp crease that ran down the
middle of her forehead, a long, slightly pointed nose. It was like the nose
on a roman coin, the nose of an emperor.

Arne shut the drawer with the side of his foot and they did not speak of it again.

She found another drawer in the bathroom. She didn't know if Arne even knew about that one.

It was in a big bureau her mom had moved there to hold towels, except that pretty soon the top drawers filled with stray buttons, coins, pens, soap samples, spools of thread; the right middle drawer with bathing suits and swim caps—suits with slimming folds and thick bras molding their tops, discarded caps with flopped rubber flowers.

Then there was the middle drawer on the left—

That drawer stuck when she pulled at its knobs. She had to tug to open it, one angled inch at a time. Inside clumped tangled loops of plastic hose, a white plastic purse, rubber blobs, a couple of thick tubes that were like toothpaste tubes only they were white and gray and metallic, a small half-opened box that held in a side compartment what looked like a little plunger, a poker-plunger, a tube and an injector.

The drawer smelled faintly of vinegar. This made sense because the only time her mom asserted complete privacy in the bathroom, the whole place reeked of vinegar. Sometimes, she even called for a bottle of it, sticking one bare arm out the door.

Les only touched the things in that drawer once. It happened after a horrible day in school when she and a group of the cool kids were sent to a room by themselves to work on an end-of-year project, which, after the cool boys slid around the room on rolling stools and the cool girls rolled long-banged eyes at them, had deteriorated into a game of hangman. Fine enough until she hadn't known the words. Stupid words. Sexy words. Words they all knew and that she insisted she did too, really she did.

She used to think she knew things–not in a smart-alecky way like Arne–but in a nice way. Now, she found she knew nothing.

At least she knew nothing about the right things: rock bands, song lyrics, drug stuff–she didn't think the other kids really knew so much drug stuff either–but they knew what all the different drugs were called, at least, and what they were supposed to do to you–

And then there was sex–as she reached for the rubber tubing, her stomach prickled, skin arched, even the house seemed to skitter–sex stuff, which was somehow connected, like the negligee, the rubber rings, to this strange poker-plunger, and, with it all, to pleasure. (Though so hard to couple with her mom, her dad, vinegar.)

She filled the poker-plunger with jell from the metallic tube. It was like a big plastic syringe, a shot without a point. Then, despite her certainty that that the mouth of the house, if not of the earth, was about to swallow her, she sat down onto the pink bathroom throw rug, straddled her legs, pulled the crotch of her shorts to one side, and pushed the plastic shot inside her, injecting its fill of beige jell.

There was no explosion. Only, after a moment, a cold and slightly slimy squishiness, pooling at her core.

So, the other kids, she thought, had been right. She was completely stupid. She knew nothing. Nothing.

Burning everywhere but the freeze between her legs, she washed the plastic shot, then put it and the metallic tube back in the drawer, looping the plastic tubing in remembered tangles, hoping that it would be some time before her mom tugged the sides open and that the plastic shot thing would have completely dried–she just couldn't squeeze a towel inside to get at the droplets–

The rest of that afternoon, she was conscious of the cold squishiness. At least, she told herself, it didn't show on the outside.

* * *

The next day, night really, Bobby Kennedy was shot.

Les stayed up late, her mom even later, watching the TV people try decide whether he'd have brain damage.

Her mom kept saying, "oh why didn't they watch him, they should have watched him," and, every once in a while, "what in the world is happening to this country?"

That was the dark pool everyone stared into. "I just can't understand what's happening to this country," one black woman wept onto the screen. "Jack, Martin, and now Bobby."

They watched the next day at school too while Bobby was being operated on. The teachers opened up the sliding wall between the two sixth grades because there was only one TV. The wall was a soft zig-zaggy thing that folded like a blubbery fan. The teachers said at the beginning of the year they'd open it all the time for special activities but, before that day, they never had.

By afternoon, there was nothing much new. The announcers just paused, voices too tired for their normal attack dog edge.

Still, it was important to keep watching, Les thought, as if watching—as if the whole country sitting there glued–could somehow pull Bobby away from the bullet.

But the other kids were being so stupid. A bunch of boys flicked a triangulated paper over fingered goalposts. Knots of girls, girls she sometimes thought of as her friends, put their heads down to cover passed notes.

Sharp splinters of light blurred at the sides of pulled shades.

"I'm tired of this," Bruce Beebee said, paper football flipping onto the floor. "Can't we just watch some cartoons?"

The boys around him tittered. The girls picked up their heads, trying both to show, and not show, smirks.

Miss Carlson bent down by his ear, cheeks crowding her whisper.

"Oh man," he said, turning from her. "I never liked the guy anyway."

Les sat up straighter so that Miss Carlson would see that at least someone was watching. She did not care that she seemed goody-goody; she did not care if she was an idiot. She remembered how, when they talked about current events, Vietnam, Bruce said that they should just bomb them all, bomb them back to the stone age

The thing was that Bobby seemed like a real person. Of course, Martin Luther King was a real person too, and JFK—

But Bobby seemed different. Like a kid; like one of his own kids. (Every once in a while, the reporters showed pictures of them playing football, blurs of teeth, hair, sweater.)

Her mom was for Humphrey, her mom who was always so right about everything–

But she knew now that she was different from her mom, that she loved Bobby, that she had loved him all along, that he was the one she had always wanted to be president.

If only, dear God, he just would be okay.

When the newsman said he had died, the teachers turned off the TV. It was time to go home anyway.

Shades snapped up like bright slaps; kids banged chairs onto desks, the loudspeaker boomed buses.

She wanted to cry, to walk arm in arm with someone and cry. She remembered JFK's—she'd been little but that's what the big kids had done—they'd been at school then too. Now, she was a big kid herself, but it wasn't what they were doing this time.

The teachers stood to the sides of the tiled hallways, grim monitors of the crowd.

Les
Suburban Maryland
Late June 1968

The sky was white the day her Uncle Duke drove up, though it was still early summer, her dad just gone for Reserves. She ran out to greet Duke's car. He smiled at her, putting his cigar in his mouth and waving both hands. It was his big smile, reaching all the way up to his eyebrows.

He wasn't her real uncle. He was her mother's cousin, maybe even second cousin, maybe even removed, whatever that meant. He was someone who'd visited her mom's family a lot when he was a kid and because they'd lived on a farm and his folks, living in a city, had a hard time taking care of him.

He hugged her with the arm that carried a small plaid suitcase.

"Mmmm," he said, picking her up. "Whew," putting her down again.

His cheeks felt smooth and rough at once, shaved and yet determined to bristle. He smelled, as always, of hair oil, cigars and some little something else–warmth–that must have been his own.

"So how's my best girl?" he said.

She smiled in a way that she was pretty sure looked cute.

"Boy, you're grown." He took a step back to look her over. "Whoowhee. And as beautiful as ever. How'd you get so pretty with a mom like that?"

He slipped his large hand over hers and they walked up the sidewalk, she skipping lightly to keep pace.

"So your mom home?"

"Yep."

"Better get rid of this then," waving his cigar stub in the air.

"You better," she laughed.

He pushed the butt of half-finished cigar into the doorstep, opened the glass door for her. She walked under his arm.

"Hey, Ingrid, I'm here. Yoo hoo," he called.

"You're here," Ingrid said, stepping up from the basement stairs, the handle of a turquoise plastic bucket in her hand. "Perfect timing. I just finished mopping up that room for you downstairs. I hope it's okay." She set the bucket down in the kitchen, sighed back into the living room.

"That's how you greet a guy? Who drives across the whole damn country to see you?!" He smiled, opening his arms. Ingrid smiled too, but reluctantly relaxed into his breadth–

"You're looking great," he said. "Lost weight?"

She hugged him for real now, laughing.

"You're the one looks great," she said.

He laughed back, then parked himself on the couch.

Les saw her mom's face tighten. She was worried, Les knew, that he was going to do something to her new upholstery. She hadn't actually let anyone sit on it so far.

Les tried to smile especially widely at Duke to make up for her mom's tension. But he didn't seem to notice Ingrid's tension; he let his weight sink down in the couch as if it were the most natural thing in the world, even stretched one arm over the sofa-back.

"So how was California then?" Ingrid asked. Her voice was calm enough, but Les could see the self-control; it was as if her mother's whole face was biting her lip. "Beautiful, doll, just beautiful. The golf courses, man. Talk about nice – they're like nothing you've ever seen."

"They're really well kept up?"

"Kept up, Christ. But it ain't a matter of the keeping up. You'll be walking around following some line drive and then here's this lemon tree" he spluttered with laughter. "Grandma would love it, gathering up those lemons, pies, lemonade, lemon pudding. I'd love to see her, stashing them in her bag, you know how she does."

"She's not as bad as all that," Ingrid said.

"I'm not saying she's bad," Duke protested. "Someone *should* collect those lemons."

"So, you drove straight here?"

"Arizona first. I had a couple of dude types out there. Boy, they were lousy golfers. Whew."

He stared at his hands a moment, but the next, looked over to Les, seeming to peek at her from under his own forehead. Then winked, eyes shining like the crinkle of cellophane off a cigar.

"Come 'ere, doll," he said. When she went over to him, he pulled her into the spread between his legs, sitting her on one knee. From there, she smelled his aftershave again, the bristly warmth now mixed with the acrid dye of the couch.

"So, how do you like my new rug?" her mom asked Duke. "And the couch? I got that chair done too."

Duke's face pulled long to look impressed. "Looks great, Ing, really classy. Must have cost a mint, huh?"

"Oh, not so much," she said. "But gosh, I deserve something nice once in a while, don't I? The way I work."

"Sure you do. Hon, you deserve something nice every single day." He winked again at Les.

"You don't think it's too dark, do you?" Ingrid's forehead creased. "The upholsterer made a mistake, used a fabric that was too dark. Then I thought maybe it was *better* dark. But now," she glared at the couch, "I just don't know again."

"Nah Ing, it's not too dark," Duke said, patting a cushion with the hand behind Les' back. "Hell, I think it's just the…just the right amount of darkness."

"If it's dark, it's dark," Ingrid sighed. "It's probably too late to return it now anyway, now that people have sat on it."

Duke smiled at Les; she tried to pass the same smile back like a secret they shared. She wasn't sure what the secret was, only that it was something about how different they were from her mother, more fun, more understanding of important things, not worried about couches.

* * *

Duke was there on a visit, but also to help out. Ingrid was busier than usual that summer–both teaching summer school in her regular elementary school and taking a university course so that she wouldn't have to teach regular elementary school anymore. So, while Les's dad was away–he had to go to Reserves for two weeks every summer–Duke was supposed to cook them breakfast, drive Les and Arne to the swimming pool, and, when they were out swimming, finish the basement.

"Finish," Les thought, was like "re-do", only in this case the basement had never been "done" in the first place, some of the walls still concrete blocks, parts of the floor cement.

Duke wasn't a real carpenter; he was a golfer, the best golfer in the world, she thought. But he was also fairly handy and needed work. (Golf didn't seem to pay so well.)

"If only he could get out of the shadow of LBJ," her mom said. They were eating dinner in the dining room because Duke was there. That part was like a guest.

Her mother was talking about Humphrey. Her mother loved Humphrey.

"He's just too nice to separate himself, that's what his problem is," she said.

"No, it isn't. His problem is that he talks too much. He can't shut up," Arne said.

Duke grunted. "That's for sure. The man's constantly running at the mouth."

"He was a teacher–you know he was first a teacher, right? Before he got to the Senate. And teachers are trained to repeat things at least three times. How do kids learn stuff you don't repeat them?" Ingrid said.

"His head is shaped like an egg," Arne said.

Duke guffawed.

"Arne," Ingrid said.

Arne didn't like Humphrey because of the war, Les thought, because he didn't think you could trust him on the war. Look at LBJ.

Her mother said that Humphrey was against the war. How could he be for war? she said.

"Humphrey Dumpty," Duke said.

"I'll get it," Les said, as the phone rang, jumping up and running down the hall to her parent's bedroom.

Her parents' bedroom was freezing because of its air conditioner.

"Mom, it's Mona," she called, then shut the door again–what they did to keep in the cold–and skipped back to the dining room. She didn't really like talk of politics but it was fun to have dinner out there, fun to have things more special, and that's what her mom always like to talk about. She passed her mom, then Arne, on the way to his room. He pinched her.

"Stop it."

"Christ, where's she off to now?" Duke said, when she got back to the table.

"It's that woman, Mona. Her friend."

"That one?" he groaned. "So, she'll be a while, huh?"

"Probably."

Irritation bristled his jaw like a second beard. "What's she talk about so long?"

"I don't know," Les shrugged. "School. The kids. Her professors."

"She always did like to gab."

"I guess so."

"Your mother? I know so."

"You want me to turn on the TV?" It sat just behind, tight now with the table opened up.

"Naw."

The kettle whistled; he cursed under his breath. Les darted into the kitchen to move it. As it yodeled to hush, she heard him clear his throat loudly, bang something.

She looked back into the dining room. He was tapping his plate with his knife.

"So, tell me Miss," he said, "they got any coffee in this joint? How about getting a man a cup of coffee?"

His face had changed. It was no longer irritated, no longer grumbling, no longer even her Uncle Duke.

"And uh–I'll take it with cream and sugar, Sugar," he said, "if you don't mind."

The back of her neck prickled. She understood immediately what he was doing. It was the waitress-customer game. They had never actually called it that but it was something they had done together since she was a little girl.

"You want me to make you coffee?" she asked. She tried to keep her face straight, to pretend not to notice that he had taken up the game. She was too big for it now. But once he'd begun, even her straight face seemed a mask, only part of her assigned role.

"That's what I'm here for," he growled. "If I wanted to make it myself, I'd 'a stayed at home."

She realized then that she'd never actually made coffee—oh she turned on the kettle, turned off the kettle, maybe even carried the cups, but not made the whole thing, not from start to finish.

She tiptoed out of the kitchen, careful that he didn't see her, and hurried down the hall to her parents' bedroom.

"Mom," she said, trying to poke through the cold blue bubble that seemed to cocoon her mom once she picked up the phone. "Duke wants some coffee."

Her mother looked up and, frowning lightly, waved her away.

Les turned quickly, purposely leaving the bedroom door open so the cold air would flow out.

"You got a problem, doll?" Duke called from the dining room.

"No."

"'Cause I'd really like to get that coffee before next week."

She hoisted herself up onto the counter opposite the stove to get a cup and saucer down from the cupboard, a pair that would match his plate. He'd want matching ones, she thought.

She looked through the shelves for something to hold the milk. Her parents didn't usually take milk in their coffee, and if they did, either poured it from the cartoon, or, if they had company, from a pitcher stored in a glass cabinet out in the dining room, a pitcher that matched her mom's best china. But she wasn't going to go out and get the good one with Duke sitting there. She didn't think her mom would want her using that one anyway.

She saw, in the middle shelf, a dark blue pitcher with silvery white speckles.

It was a pitcher her dad, the pancake and waffle maker in their house, used when he decided to heat the syrup.

As she pulled it free from the cupboard, she pressed her face into the brilliant white porcelain inside, sniffing for maply sweetness. The pitcher smelled of cold only and the waxen dust of shelf paper. She smiled, placing it by her knees, and jumped to the floor, bare feet landing with a slap.

"Hey, what's going on in there?" Duke called. "I don't want to have to clean up any dead bodies."

"You won't," she giggled.

"And another thing—" his voice deepening—"could you make it a little snappier?"

She dipped a spoon into the instant coffee jar, adjusting the level of granules back and forth to what seemed like the amount her mother used for a cup, then carefully poured the boiling water. As she poured, she held her body as far away as she could from the steaming stream, arm tensed.

A splotchy foam bubbled to the surface of the cup. That looked wrong at first, but then it seemed to her she'd seen it in her mom's coffee too. She stirred quickly, but silently, careful not to hit the spoon against the sides of the cup.

"Uh... Miss," he said.

"Just a second."

She hurried to get the milk out, carrying the container with two hands, closing the refrigerator with her leg.

Midnight blue, that's what that color was called.

She felt so happy pouring the white shiny milk into the white shiny inside of the night sky pitcher, sniffing steaming coffee in matching cup and saucer. She felt silly to be so happy, still happy.

She carried the cup and saucer to him slowly, her gait as intensely straight as a would-be dancer balancing a book on her head.

"Aha!" Duke's smile broadened with the coffee smell. Then just as quickly, he turned insistent again. "Hey where's the milk?"

"Coming."

"Ah," as she brought in the pitcher. He leaned back from the table so she could pour. "That's more like it."

"You want sugar?"

"Sure, one spoon. You do the honors."

She got the sugar bowl from the glass cabinet in the dining room. She wasn't used to spooning sugar; she felt her hand tremble as she measured it, though he didn't seem to notice anything except for the amount of sugar she was putting in.

Because he waited for her to stir, she stirred.

"Sorry it took so long," she hazarded.

"Darn right," he said. "How's this place going to stay in business, service like that?"

His lower lip protruded like he was really mad. But the next moment, his jaw creased upward.

"My, that coffee smells good. Even for instant. And you've done it all so nice."

Cupping one arm and hand around her waist, he pulled her to him. With the other hand he raised the cup and took a sip.

"Boy, that hits the spot."

After another sip, he leaned back into the red velvet back of the chair (he always sat on her mom's fanciest one, the one that normally sat against the wall as a kind of decoration) so that she was pulled half off her feet. She pressed her hand against his side to balance herself. Beneath her fingertips she could feel the softness of his flesh through his shirt. The flesh felt like flannel over his ribs, a second shirt.

What she was most conscious of again was his smell—ketchup combined with shaving cream, that burnt cold smell of coffee, the sour rotting sweetness of old cigars, and beneath it all, that intense warmth. Being next to him was like being next to a motor.

"So tell me, doll," he said, nudging her towards him with the crook of his arm. "What time you get off work tonight?"

She laughed awkwardly.

"Huh?" nudging her back. "Eleven, twelve? I can wait, you know. I got all the time in the world for a girl like you."

The way he held her was uncomfortable, but she worried that moving would hurt his feelings. Too close to look at him, she focused on the table–Arne's plate was smeared with the sticky remains of ketchup, her own lightly crusted with the pink crumbs of burger, curls of iceberg lettuce.

How could her mother talk on the phone so long? Just leave Duke–when he was a guest, sort of.

She looked at the pitcher, trying to pour herself into that blur of midnight blue and starlight speckle.

"I don't know," she said.

As Les carried the dishes in to the sink—it was the kind of thing girls did–Duke moved out to the kitchen. Arne came slogging down the hall, the sports pages dragging from one hand like a pet on a leash.

"You could help too," she told him.

"No, I couldn't," Arne said. "Anything else to eat?" He bent down into the refrigerator, took out a small cantaloupe and, carrying it over to the counter, cut it in two. Scooped out the seeds of one half, plopped it in a bowl and sat down at the table.

"Hey Arne, that's too much. There are other people here, you know."

"You want some?" he said, spreading out the sports pages. "Take the other half."

"Arne!" she said. But her voice, with Duke listening, sounded to her like a caricature of an exasperated TV mother. She flushed.

"Don't mind him," Duke said, touching her shoulder. "He's a growing boy and all that–"

"Yeah, well what about me?" Les said. "Aren't I growing? What about you?"

Duke patted his middle. "I may be growing all right, but it's not something I want to encourage."

"He shouldn't take it all."

"Let him take it. You take the other half. I don't like that melon stuff, you know me. And your mom's lost all rights." He looked up to the clock. "Geez, what the hell does that woman talk about so long?"

Les cut a piece from the remaining half of the melon for herself. A part of her did feel like taking her mother's piece. But even though Duke said she should do it, he might not think it very nice if she actually did.

They were quiet now, except for Arne's chomping. It amazed her that he could be so oblivious. Of course, he was a boy. Boys didn't have to be nice, to even think about being nice, especially him.

She tried to eat her melon delicately in case Duke watched her. But he was reading the backs of the sports pages Arne leafed through. No, now he was checking out things on the kitchen wall.

"So, what's this?" he asked, squinting into the calendar. "'Arne Acolyte Sunday July 16.' Hey, Arne, you one of those guys in the robes?"

It was her dad's handwriting. He had scrawled it on the calendar so Arne wouldn't forget, pretend to forget, while he was away.

Arne scowled, shook out the newspaper, turned the page.

"Arne, I can't hear you," Duke sang out.

"Dad makes him do it," Les said. "It's only six more times."

"Four," Arne muttered.

"Four? No–," she said.

"Sure, it's four more. I did it in March, April, May, June."

"Oh yeah. Okay, four more."

"So, four more and then what? You graduate?" Duke asked.

"No, silly. He made a deal with Dad, see, that if he did it six more times, he wouldn't have to do it anymore. And now he's done two of them."

"You mean I won't have to go to church at all anymore," Arne said loftily. "That's what the deal is. Not just being an acolyte."

"Won't go to church at all," Duke said. "Aw, come on Arne. I can't believe your Dad would make a deal like that. Not the Dad I know. You gotta go to church sometimes."

"Do you go to church?" Arne asked.

Duke put his hand over his mouth in a silent "oh-oh".

"But hey, let's be serious," he said. "You don't want to be like me. Look at your Dad, going to church every week, even a big scientist like him–"

"Going to coffee hour for the home-made cookies," Les giggled.

"Go to hell," Arne said.

"Come on, Arne, don't be like that," Duke said. "And by the way, I *do* go to church sometimes. You should see me back in old Minnesota. I get dressed up. Grandma gets fancy. I take her uptown in the car." His eyes focused sentimentally into the distance. "I always think 'Christ, I gotta do this more often."

"Course you never do," Arne said.

"Well, no," Duke sighed. "At least not as much as I should."

Arne turned back to the sports pages, but Duke, with fingertips only, pulled them lightly away, then held them behind his back.

"So let's be serious. How's about I take you tomorrow? I'd kinda like to see you all dressed up. You know–Angel Arne." He spread his arms out to the side, smiling goofily.

"You too, Angel," looking over to Les. "Angel Angel," he smiled. "That's what I'll call you."

Arne scowled.

"Oh come on, Arne, what about it? Christ, if I can take you to the horse races, I can take you to church, can't I? Your mom can sleep late, work on her paper. Your dad–he can rest assured. By the way, where is he this year?"

"Reserves," Les said.

"I know he's in Reserves–I mean, where Reserves?"

"South Carolina," Arne said. "Or maybe, I don't know, North."

"Glad you guys are keeping such close track," Duke said.

* * *

The house was quiet when she woke. It felt early, the light that angle-less pitch of morning, summers. It was going to be hot though, she could tell that much, the air, though still fresh, like the side of a block that held a drycleaner's, laden with oncoming heat.

She felt sure Duke had forgotten about church, that last night's talk been part of his typical bluster.

She lay flat on her back and stretched, her feet seeking out the cool places hiding in the corners of her bed. She wondered whether she should wake up her mother, remind her of the acolyte business, or wait and see if Arne was going to tell her.

Just as she was deciding that she would definitely rather not wake her mom, she heard Duke's heavy step on the basement stairs, in the hallway then right there, at her door. His hair freshly oiled and combed looked starkly black, a curve of night sky against a face that was unusually haggard, a chunk of pocked moon.

"Rise and shine. Time to get up. Hey Les, Arne, come on, time's awastin'."

The gray face was something of a lie. He grinned broadly now, in his parade mode, the Music Man.

He swept over to her closet door and scraped the dress hangers across the rod.

She covered her ears.

"I can pick something out myself," she said.

Arne groaned from the room across the hall. "What time is it?"

"Time to get your heinie out of bed," Duke called.

"Uncle Duke—" Les said.

"Oops," Duke covered his mouth. "Time to wake up darling," he said, switching to falsetto.

She laughed and pulled the sheet up over her face.

He swept it off with one hand. In the other, he held up a pale pink lace dress, her Easter dress from the year before.

"Here."

"But Uncle Duke—"

"Don't 'Uncle Duke' me. If I'm taking you to church, the least you can do is look your best."

"Do I have to go to church?" she asked.

"What do you mean do you have to go to church? I'm taking you, aren't I?"

"I mean, can I just go to Sunday School?"

"Oh Jesus Christ. Sunday School, church–just get dressed will you?"

"Okay, but uh–" she smiled slyly. "Uncle Duke?"

"Huh?"

"That dress is too small."

He tossed it onto the bed. "Look at you, ten years old, a whole decade. Aren't you old enough to dress yourself yet?"

"Sure I am. And I'm eleven actually. Just turned."

"Christ. So, just do it then," he said. "But none of that shorts stuff. What do you call them?"

She thought a minute. "Culottes?"

"Yeah, none of those. Not when I'm taking you. Not even to Sunday School."

"Yes sir," she said, saluting.

"That's more like it."

As he huffed off to badger Arne, she jumped out of bed, shut the door. She found this year's Sunday dress and put it on quickly. Through the door, she could hear Duke shouting a battery of commands. She laughed.

Normally, she spent mornings, at least a part of them, in her mom's bed. She would scamper in there first thing and squeeze in behind her mom, feeling deliciously little. It wasn't that her mother was so big, but in the mornings, her body seemed swollen with the night before, weighted with the sky bulk of sheet and covers, the gray blinded windows, her own sleep breath.

She loved this coziness any morning, but on Sundays, her feelings were a little more calculated. On Sundays, she tried to become such an integral part of her mother's sleep web that her dad, who was in charge of Sunday School and church, would have to disturb her mom to get her going. Which, she knew, was something he wouldn't want to do.

It wasn't that Ingrid never went to church. But her going was an ordeal. Her glare, when pulled out of bed early, swung about like a spotlight, finding fault, demanding perfection, and if perfection was impossible, she could at least take a moment to get mad about life as it was.

Careful of her mother's door, Les snuck down the hall to the bathroom, then into the kitchen for some cereal.

Duke stood at the sink, cleaning his coffee cup.

"You ready?" he asked. "Your brother okay?"

"I don't know." She leaned against the counter so she could jump up on it, get a bowl down from the cupboard.

"Hey, what do you think you're doing? You're going to rip your dress doing that."

"No, I'm not."

"Well, put your shoes on. And get your brother moving. I tell you one thing about going with your Uncle Duke, you're not going to have a ripped dress and you're not going to be late."

"I'm hungry."

"You may be hungry, but you won't be late."

As she went back to her room to get her dress shoes, she passed the bathroom door, shut now.

She gave the door a bang. "Arne, hurry up."

"Leave me alone."

After she put her shoes on, she slipped through the door of her parents' bedroom.

It could be any season, any time of day. Any time of night really. Her mother, a tangle of sheet and nightgown, lay asleep, eyelids smooth, the line that bisected her forehead relaxed.

Les pranced lightly across the floor, then jumped onto her mother's mattress, landing on her knees just beside her.

"Huh.... oh Les. Don't," her mom said, turning and pulling up some of the sheet Les had caught. Then, abruptly, she pulled herself up, peering towards the clock. "Oh my gosh, what time is it?"

Les swayed back, checking. "8:05."

"Oh dear.... What time is Arne supposed to be there?"

"No, it's okay. Duke's up. You know he said he would take us? Well, he is."

"He is, huh? Good for him." Ingrid lay back down. "So you set?" She opened her eyes. "Arne find a shirt okay?"

"I guess so."

"I better go and check."

"No, he's okay."

"He's probably got an old wrinkled one."

"He's going to have that robe on anyhow," Les said. "Can't see his shirt."

"That's true. But you can see his collar."

"Nah. Anyway he'd tell you, Mom, or Duke would. He's as bad about clothes as you."

"Mmmm. I guess Duke would tell me." Her mom turned toward the wall, folding back into sleep. "Have a good time, sweetie."

The turning of her mother filled Les with a sudden ache. She wished now she hadn't avoided the door earlier. She wished she had scurried in there like she did every Sunday, like she did almost every single morning, had wrapped herself in that crumpled softness, refrigerated warmth.

She stopped swaying on her knees and lay down next to her mom, on her side at first, and then to avoid wrinkling her dress, on her back. She positioned her legs diagonally, so that her shoes hung over the side of the mattress not touching the sheets. They were her good shoes anyway, cleanish on the bottoms.

"Les, honestly," her mother said, pulling the sheet more tightly around her shoulder. "I don't want to have to iron that dress too now."

"Iron that dress *too*–"

"Les–" Duke's gravely voice called down the hall. "You ready?"

She got up, hand flashing over tears.

Her mom turned over towards her. "Listen, sweetie. You know in that drawer, the one under the books."

Les knew the drawer.

"Can you just get ten dollars and give it to Duke? If he has to make some kind of offering, or, I don't know, take you guys out afterwards—"

"Okay."

Les reached into the drawer for the money envelope, took out a ten, then carefully put the envelope back and shut the drawer.

"I got it."

"Great," her mom said.

Duke and Arne waited at the front door. Duke had put a plaid sports jacket on and was retying Arne's tie. Arne was pulling away from him, twisting his neck to the side.

"Stop that," Duke said. "You want me to do this or don't you?"

"I don't."

"Well, I'm gonna anyway," Duke said. "You can't go out all which way. You gotta get the bottom half to lay flat under the top half—there— Don't your dad teach you anything?"

At first, when Duke first took his hand away, the tie lay flat, as if mesmerized by his touch. Then the knot turned defiantly askew.

"Forget it," Arne said, breaking from Duke's grasp. "I'll get a fake one."

"Well, hurry up about it." Duke turned to the mirror to adjust his own tie.

Arne rolled his eyes at Les. Les giggled.

Now, Duke turned to her, inspecting. She pivoted slightly to each side.

He breathed out a soft wolf's whistle. "You look great doll, good enough to eat." He growled, his hands curled by the sides of his face like claws.

She laughed. "Here," handing over the ten. "This is from my mom. In case you want to make an offering or something, or go out afterwards."

"Isn't that nice of her?" He slipped the bill into his pocket, looked down at his watch.

"Arne, dearie," he called. "Your mom may be late as hell Arne, but your Uncle Duke is not."

Silence.

Duke, assuming his joke face, motioned "sshhh" to Les, finger over his lips. "We're leaving now Arne." He pressed his feet hard into the carpet, the exaggerated gesture of the mime. "Yup, you'll be home here looking at Playboys, Arne, and there won't be anyone to light the candles." He opened the door and without stepping outside, clanked it shut.

Arne came around the corner of the hallway in a rush, cheeks pink, hand clamping the tie into the corners of his shirt collar.

"Aha, got you." Duke laughed. "Come on doll. Heaven's waiting."

Les dashed back to the hallway, shouted, "bye-bye mom," then hurried out past Arne, skipping down the walk to the car.

"So, what makes you so picky about church?" Arne asked, as the car wheeled down the street.

"Who says I'm picky?" Duke said.

"Aw, come off it–you know what with wearing this and that. Getting the tie right. Since when did you start caring about ties?"

"I've always cared about ties," Duke protested.

"I mean, caring about my tie."

"You're my nephew, Arne. Or something like that. Whatever you are, I'm here to help take care of you in place of your dad while he's off doing his war duties." He paused, waiting for a laugh.

Arne laughed, but Les wished Duke wouldn't say that. She didn't quite understand what "reserves" was—the word always reminded her of jam. She knew that it had nothing to do with jam, but she couldn't imagine it having anything to do with war either. Not her father. "No, but serious," Duke went on, "shouldn't I want you to look the way you're supposed to? Don't I have a right, hey, an ob-li-ga-tion, to take an interest in something like that?

"Look, the way I figure it's like this. There are some things in life you only get one chance at, so you don't want to blow 'em, right? It's like when I'm on the putting green and there's that little white ball and that little black hole–I'm not going to get a chance to take ten shots at it, at least I don't want to take ten shots at it. That's blowing it."

Arne groaned, "Jesus Christ. This is church we're talking about."

"Cut the crap too, Arne."

"Now what?"

"You know what I mean. All that J.C. here and there."

"J.C.? Wait a minute, aren't I speaking to Mr. J.C. himself."

"Shucks. You keep holding me up like I'm supposed to be perfect. I'm not perfect, okay? Pretty damn close," he smiled wolfishly, "but not 100%. So, not on the way to church, okay? Pretend your mouth is a liquor store. Closed on Sundays."

Arne rolled his eyes again. Les laughed. She wasn't completely sure what they were talking about, but she took Duke's side. It *was* important to look nice, talk nice, be nice. Though it was also a little crazy to do it just on Sundays. God was supposed to know what you were doing all the time. He was kind of like Santa Claus, only a real one. It was like He had a secret camera, able to see you even if you were sitting there going to the bathroom, changing your clothes. He knew if you couldn't tie your tie right or gambled or if your house was a mess. So, it seemed a little nutty to only try to be good some of the time.

She watched Duke drive, trying to find in the nod of his neck, the shape of the side of his jaw something of her mother, only of course everything was thicker and broader and heavier than on her mother, and the skin darker, yellower in some places, redder in others. He was more lined than her mother too, at least on the back of his neck. And they weren't honestly very closely related.

"So, what does this have to do with getting dressed for church?" Arne asked.

Duke sneered. "You're a smart boy Arne, studying all that probability all the time. Just you think a little bit–just you think the whole thing through."

It was a new church, a modern design. A hugely tall triangular roof over a squat cinderblock base, all sitting upon the flat desolation of recent construction.

Duke stopped the car, but made no motion to get out. Arne and Les waited.

The parking lot was not crowded. They must be pretty early after all.

Arne finally muttered something Les didn't understand and got out.

"Uncle Duke, I was just kidding this morning about Sunday School," she said quietly. "I'll keep you company at the service if you want."

"Huh?" He said, then seemed to shake himself into alertness. "Oh. Ah, you go ahead to Sunday School, doll, if that's what you want, and you, Arne." Arne was hovering several paces from the car. "You hurry up and get into those robes. The whole thing has to wait for you, right? My land, boy, get going."

Les moved out of the car slowly. "You know," she said, coming over to Duke's window. "You can go somewhere and come back for us. You don't have to wait out here."

He smiled up at her. "You just run along, sweetcakes. I still haven't made up my mind I don't want to go take a peep at Angel Arne over there—"

"You can do that," Les said. "Honest. You can go for the whole thing or just a little bit. Nobody will pay attention to you at the early service."

Duke leaned back from the window in a cartoon double take. "Nobody will pay much attention to me! Whoa, what's the point of going if the minister ain't even going to mark it down in his little black book?"

Les flushed.

"Just kiddin'," he said, tapping her wrist. "Listen, sweetheart, don't worry about me, okay? It's only what? Forty-five minutes? An hour? You just go along."

She started off slowly.

"Go on now, doll," he said, and, feeling this push to be genuine, she began to run lightly, her white patent leather shoes clicking against the gravel that dusted the fresh blacktop.

Arne was waiting for her at the heavy metal doors. "He's such a fake," he hissed.

* * *

Her Sunday School class was in the basement. She sat on a metal folding chair. The teacher talked about Jonah, Jonah and the great fish. "Only we would call it a whale," she said.

It was hard to listen. She wished that Duke had gone to church with her. He probably wouldn't let her draw pictures on the program like her parents did. Still, to hear him try to sing, to see him roll his eyes as the sermon went on too long, give her hand a squeeze—

She looked down at her hands. She had found some white gloves at the last minute and, for Duke's sake, had worn them. The seams crawled around her fingertips like little railroad tracks, worn and grimy.

She took the gloves off.

She was hungry too. He hadn't even let them get breakfast.

She ran her white patent leather shoes against the yellow and white tiles. In their basement at home they had square tiles too, only theirs were black and white. Her mother had put them down before Duke had come. On her knees over the raw concrete, she had glued the small squares with the intense concentration that was habitual with her, not letting anyone help for fear they wouldn't get it right.

The windows were like their basement windows too. High in the walls. Grass showing.

It was as if they were buried down there and up above was Arne floating long and serious in his white and black robes. An angel, like Duke said, a stupid angel.

Out in the sunshine, in the real world, was Duke. Leaning into the gleam of his car, yawning.

Though probably he didn't wait. Probably he had gone off to a coffee shop already, Les thought, joking with some waitress.

She felt her face grow hot.

The teacher, in the midst of talking of how Jonah prayed for God's help, got very quiet and gave the boys in the back a dirty look.

When it was finally over, she hurried up the stairs. She wasn't mad at Duke now. Mainly worried. It had been so long. And he wasn't like her dad, someone who was willing to wait forever. He was what her mother called the "he-man" type, the kind of man you couldn't make wait, the kind who got mad.

Whoa, it was bright out. Where was he?

She was just sinking into the thought that he'd gone and not come back when she found him, standing right by his car.

She walked towards him, waiting for him to notice her.

But he wasn't even looking out for her. Every time someone walked by, which was beginning to happen more often as the next service approached, he flashed them a big full-faced greeting.

Les knew this greeting. She'd seen it out in the mid-west when he met farmers and their wives in town. She always thought he saved it for people he considered simple-minded.

"Howdy!" "Well hello there!" "How *are* you?" She couldn't actually hear Duke, but this was what he seemed to say, his smile clenched but animated.

It all seemed so fake to her, a big fat joke. But a lot of the church-goers not only smiled back at Duke, they stopped to talk to him, even waited so they could walk to the church doors together, until he shrugged, made some kind of excuse.

It made her uncomfortable to see him acting like that with people who were really her parents' people. She darted across the parking lot.

"Hey doll," he said, pressing the hand she gave him to his chest. "So how did it go, huh? You put in a few good words for your Uncle Duke?"

She blushed.

"I need all the help I can get," he said, squatting to her level.

"Hey Arne," he said, standing up.

Arne was just behind her, face sullen.

"Oh, come on, Arne," Les said. "Don't be such a teenager."

"I am a teenager."

"You tell her Arne," Duke said.

As Arne got into the back seat, Duke winked at Les, took her hand and led her to the other side of the car, where he opened the front door for her and bowed, "at your service, Madam."

She clambered, embarrassed, past him, then began climbing over the seat to get in back.

"Hey, where you going?" he said. "You sit up here next to me. I need some of that good stuff to rub off."

"Did you stay outside the whole time?"

"Me? Hell no. First, I paid the pastor a little visit. In chambers, as they say. Then I took a peek at Angel Arne back there."

Arne, lounging in back, straightened up slightly.

"Did you really?" Les asked.

"Sure, I really. I didn't get all dressed up just to match the car, did I?"

"If you came in, where did you sit?" Arne asked.

"Do I sense a lack of faith in the gallery?" Duke eyed him in the mirror.

"If you came in to see me, I just want to know that's all."

"Questions, questions. What a man does in a church is his own private business. Haven't you never heard that before, a smart boy like you?"

Arne shrugged again. Les laughed.

"Well, kids," Duke said, "now we've had our religion for the day, I'm in the mood for a cup of coffee and a doughnut. Anyone want to join me?"

"I do," Les said.

"Okay with you, Arne?"

"If you want."

"Look, Arne," Duke stuck his free hand back over the seat. "You're a real sport, you know that? Going along with all this stuff to please your dad. You're a real good kid."

"Come on Arne," Les said.

Duke stretched his hand further back.

"Thanks," Arne said, limply touching hands over the seat.

"Now, isn't there a donut shop someplace in these here parts?"

Dunkin' Donuts was made of glass. It reminded Les of Dulles Airport, a big glass bird of a building. She knew it was silly to compare a donut shop to an airport, still the shop's glass, reflecting blue and black and brilliance in the sun, gave her that same strange lift.

The hut was highly air-conditioned. Les's fancy dress, which had grown stickily close in the car, backed away from her arms, her neck, her back. She rubbed her bare arms softly in the chill.

There was only one waitress, a young woman, who, except for eyes encircled in black, was all silver and lavender, even her hair, which was teased into a stiff, puffy french twist.

Frosted hair, frosted lips, frosted eyeshadow. It was a look her mother always called "not very natural".

Duke smiled at the waitress. Did he wink? Les wasn't sure but thought he probably had, or would anyway. Winking was what he did with waitresses.

"Hey doll. Beautiful girl for a beautiful day," he said.

Les always felt a little catch at the beginning of these things–was the waitress going to like it or was she going to get mad?

"My gosh, you've got a lot of doughnuts here," Duke went on, "Did you make all those yourself? Boy, you must be one talented girl."

The waitress crossed her arms, which worried Les, then smiled.

"No sir," she said, "They do make 'em back there, but not me."

Arne put his head on the counter over his folded arms and shut his eyes.

"Arne! Wake up!" Duke said, shaking Arne's arm. "You'll have to excuse the boy, Miss. He's had a big day already."

Les watched the waitress. The black around her eyes was not natural, but it was pretty. It made her eyes look like deer eyes–the female deer in *Bambi*. They even looked a little like Twiggy's eyes, Les thought, except with her tall sculptured hair, and the lavender uniform, tight over her breasts, the woman didn't really look like Twiggy.

"Cheryl" tugged one breast in perfectly sewn red script.

Her tendrils were the best, Les thought, little curls that shook but still held firm, each one like a set of silver rings you could put your finger up.

"You'll have to excuse him Cheryl," Duke said, holding Arne's sleeve. "Do you mind if I call you Cheryl? I'm Duke and this here is Angel–" Arne roused quickly at that, jerking his arm away. "Excuse me, this here is Mr. Arne, my nephew, and my niece, Leslie, *Miss* Leslie."

"Hi Mr. Arne," the waitress said smiling at him.

"So what'll it be, kid?" Duke asked him. "You're still too young for coffee but I'm not sure you couldn't use a drop."

"I'll take a glazed," Arne said. "No," leaning to look around Duke, to read the little signs at the base of the trays. "A honey-dipped."

'Glazed' was they were called at the places they used to go to, when there were hardly any stores out here, and they had to drive into the city to buy something. It was like frozen custard. In the city it had been called frozen custard, but now they had it out here, it was soft ice cream. Soft ice cream sounded okay, Les thought, but "honey-dipped" seemed fake, as if they thought they could really fool people into thinking it was honey they dipped the doughnuts in, as if people nowadays were so stupid, people in the suburbs.

Les got up and went to the part of the counter where she could see the doughnuts better.

"You made up your mind, sweetcakes?" Duke seemed both to turn to Les and smile at the waitress at once. "It's a big decision."

Les felt her cheeks burn, conscious of a camaraderie between Duke and the waitress, some joke.

"Oh, come on, Les," Arne groaned.

"Okay, okay, apple cinnamon," she said.

"Apple cinnamon, that's sort of like apple pie, right?" Duke asked, then turned back to Les. "So, you like that? You want one that tastes like apple pie in the middle?"

She nodded, face reddening.

"Great. So, one cinnamon apple–make that one of the big ones, right? And one–hmmmm... Now, Cheryl, you're telling me you didn't make a single doughnut?"

The waitress shook her head, truly smiling this time.

"Not a one?" he moaned.

Cheryl laughed. "No sir."

"Then how about one of those old-fashions? 'Cause you know," he drew something with his finger on the counter, "I guess I'm kind of an old fashioned guy."

The waitress picked up the doughnuts with squares of tissue paper. "You'll have coffee with that?" she asked.

"You're a mind reader too, huh? Light, if it's not too much trouble."

The coffee black, the metal cream pitcher, the sugar–

Duke gave the waitress his big set grin, his teeth big and close together, white corn on the cob.

Les felt a sudden remorse. She didn't think she could ever be this kind of pale, black-eyed blonde, with lots of hair and makeup. She somehow felt sure that even when she grew up she'd always be "natural" in that way her mother liked, the navy blue lines of sensible.

The only make-up her mother wore was a deep tan foundation she put on with wet toilet paper and bright pink or red lipstick. No eyeliner, shadow. No eyelashes, fingernails. Her hair wavy from curlers she put in herself.

Even though Les felt very different from her mother, thinner, with even features, a not-long nose, she didn't think she would be able to make the jump to teased hair, thick eyeliner, semi-permanent tendrils.

"Hey sugar, you want to do the honors?" Duke said, turning to her.

He meant pouring the cream. She smiled; she blushed. She got up on her knees on her stool to reach the little cream pot more easily.

"Just till it's like smoke," he said, as she began to pour, and "there," when the milk marbleized.

"Yech–these are always so sweet," Arne said, dropping a nearly finished doughnut to the napkin with a look of disgust.

"I can see how much you hated it," Duke said.

"Okay," Arne smiled, licking a smear of glaze from his lower lip. "But could I have some orange juice?"

"Sure, kid, sure. What about you, doll?"

Les paused. It seemed wrong to make Duke spend more money on them; she didn't think he had much money. Then she remembered the ten.

"Some milk maybe?" he nudged. "Looks like it would go with that."

"Okay."

He put his finger up for the waitress, engineered his big-toothed smile.

"Sorry to trouble you, ma'am–"

Had he forgotten her name already?

"Cheryl," Les whispered.

* * *

When they got home from Dunkin' Donuts, her mother was lying on the couch looking at the Sunday paper.

"I'm just sick of that paper," she said. "I can't think about it one more minute."

Les knew that when she talked of the paper she was sick of, she didn't mean the newspaper, which she returned to almost instantly, but the one she was working on for her course.

A paper didn't sound like a big deal, but since her mom had gone back to school last year, Les had come to understand that it was not what it sounded like. It was tons and tons of papers—pages, anyway. Her mom said she'd never be able to do it. What they wanted was so stupid, she said.

"Just take a break," Arne said.

"Yeah mom," she said.

"You're not behind, are you?" Duke began to unwrap a cigar–

"Sweetheart," Ingrid said, with grim directness. "Do you have to do that in here?"

"Jesus Christ, woman."

"I'm sorry," she said, "but there's the whole downstairs, the whole back yard–"

"By jiminy...." His face tightened, puffed up slightly, then reined itself in again. "Christ," he said.

They heard the bulk of him tread down the stairs to the basement, the creaking swing of the backdoor.

"Oh god," her mother said.

Les looked at her. Arne squatted down over the newspaper.

"Well, gee," Ingrid went on defensively, "does he have to spread that smell all over the house? I mean every single room?"

Arne shrugged—"the man smokes cigars."

"I just want to preserve *one* area. Is that so terrible?"

They heard the sound of the backdoor slamming. Ingrid sat up sharply and looked out the window behind the couch, straining to find Duke in the backyard. Les kneeled on the couch next to her, also looking out.

Ingrid sat forward again. "Okay, so I'm terrible," she said. "After he took you to church and everything. And he's taking you to the swim team every single morning too. And working so hard on the basement."

"He's been picking us up too," Les said. "And that wall he built for the closet is really nice."

"Here, look–" Ingrid turned back to her. "You want to go tell him I'm sorry..." She put her hand on her forehead. "Oh darn it, let him smoke up the whole damn house, I don't care." She sighed, shook her head, picked up the newspaper, though she didn't look at it yet. She looked out the window again, only this time towards the sky. "Hey, let's go to the pool, okay? I've just got to get outside a little. Listen," back to Les, "you want to ask him to come?"

"You'll think he'll want to?" Les asked. "He never comes with us."

"I don't know, but just ask him, huh? Be nice."

Les ran to the basement stairs and, holding the railing, jumped several at a time.

"Duke?"

No answer.

"Du-uke?"

She stopped in the middle of the stairwell. She hated the downstairs. It sometimes scared her just to just walk over from the bottom of the stairs to the backdoor, and they were practically next to each other. She used to imagine that if she stepped on a line of the tile down there, a shark would bite her feet, or an alligator.

Maybe it would be better when it was finished. Especially if Duke managed to block out the cellar part, the dark side where the washer and dryer sat, and the old boxes they carried down whenever someone was coming to visit and they tried to clean everything up upstairs.

Whenever she had to go to that area of the basement, she would run, jumping the clothes into the dryer or from the dryer to a laundry basket, racing back up the stairs, imagining that she was being chased by gorillas, partly to speed herself up, partly because she felt as if she really was. (Though she knew that wasn't true, really she knew that.)

"Duke?" she tried again, taking the last few steps down.

"Here I am, sweetcakes—"

The screen door scratched against the floor.

"Out here."

It was hot on the patio and so bright she could see the edge of her own nose.

He sat in an old plastic lawn chair. His suit jacket looked metallic against the plastic, outlined by the white-hot stucco of the patio. His face, his neck, outlined by suit jacket looked old. Wrinkles she'd never noticed sagged from his neck into the smooth cloth of his collar, so that his face seemed pieced together like a collage, odd pictures glued on top of each other.

"Mom says she's sorry. She didn't mean it. She says you can smoke wherever you want.... But," she added in a more confidential tone of voice, "you know how she is about the upstairs. Especially since she got all the furniture re-done."

He nodded, exhaling a cloud of cigar. "Yeah, I know your mother."

They were both silent, looking into the green sprawl of untrimmed forsythia bush. He put his arm around Les, rubbed his bristly chin against her upper arm. She pulled her arm away from the sting, but then tried to relax, just let it happen, the rubbing something he seemed to like.

His suit, her turquoise Easter dress—were they what made the whole thing seem so strange? His eyes creased as he squinted out the sun. She thought of the paper fans she used to make, folding and refolding little accordions. Arne's paper airplanes.

Duke sighed. "Yep, I know your mother. I've known her my whole damn life." He chuckled. "Well, a lot of it. I got a few years free..... Hah!" He let go of Les' arm to take a drag of his cigar.

"She was a real stinker," he said. Another drag. He sighed and looked back to her.

"But not you doll. Nope. You were always a dream, even as a little baby." He smiled. "I'd come and take care of you, this little red thing. I don't know how she got so lucky."

"Les–" She heard her mother call from upstairs. "You ready?"

Les broke away from him. "Look," she said. "We're going to the swimming pool and Mom wants to know if you'll come. You don't have to," she said, "but you might like it. They have food and a fancy bar and all kinds of stuff. You don't have to just swim."

"Food and a bar and all kinds of stuff" he mocked. "What about bathing beauties; they got any bathing beauties?"

She blushed. What he wanted her to say, she knew, was that they had her, but all she could do was laugh.

Because they were going. And he was coming. And it was sure to be so much fun.

"Anyway, you guys are so hot against the war," Duke said from over his shoulder, driving, "you should love Nixon. He's got a plan to end it."

Because her mom was coming, and it was Sunday, they went to the fancy pool at the officers' club, and not to the closer pool they used for everyday.

They were members of the officers' club because, Les thought, of her dad's Reserves. So that was one good thing about it. He had also fought in World War II and in the Korean War, or been "called up" in the Korean War, she didn't think he'd fought exactly. But she also didn't think that being in the wars necessarily got you into the officers' club anyway. Because Duke had fought in World War II and had even caught malaria. But she was pretty sure he couldn't have joined.

"Nixon!" Ingrid cried. "Duke, you can't tell me you're Mr. Republican now."

"Christ, Ing, since when have I not been Mr. Republican—ever since I was old enough to think on my own."

"You don't have the money to be a Republican, don't you know that, sweetie?"

"Mom, please," Les said.

"Ssh, baby, this is important now," Duke said, turning completely from the road to look back at her. "Your mom thinks your political party is a matter of money, when really it's who you are, what you think. Now, what I think is that those Democrats are full of –okay let's call it hot air, how about that?" Duke had turned back to the road, but now winked at Les in the rear view mirror. "Seein' as little Les is here."

"A secret plan to end the war," Arne smirked. "And it just happens to have occurred to him right before the election."

"When better?" Duke laughed.

"I think," Les said, leaning up towards the front seat, "that if Nixon has some great plan to end the war, then he should just tell it. He should go see Johnson right now and put it to work."

"Don't be silly, Les," Duke said, still peering at her in the rear view. "He can't do that."

"Why not? If he's got such a great plan?"

"It's politics, see. You come up with a plan, you don't go giving it away. It's just like baseball. You don't go telling the other side all your signals and everything. Things just don't work that way."

"But if people are dying."

"Oh, come on, sweetheart."

"I don't think he's got a secret plan anyway," Ingrid said. "I think his plan is just to try to win the election. Then he's just going to bomb some more, bomb 'em to hell."

"Well, that's something, aint it?" Duke said.

The officers' club was on a military base. There was a small checkpoint at the entrance. The soldiers usually just waved cars through and saluted, but the soldier on their side stopped them now because they had used Duke's car and he didn't have the right stickers. When her mom showed the pool cards, the soldier saluted them.

"Damn right," Duke said, saluting back.

Now, her mother sat by the side of the pool, reading the Sunday magazine and throwing a dime in the water. Les went after it, jumping above the surface of the water. Then she flipped over, diving down with the imagined straightness of a spear.

In the water, the coin looked like a planet, a picture taken from one of the Gemini space shots, luminous. The side of the pool was painted aqua; the blue made the water look like a sea seen from a distance.

She liked to pretend the dime was a diamond. Though there was a certain thrill in catching it mid-sink, she also didn't mind missing it and having to scan the pool's bottom, pressing her arms into a weightless wriggling dance, an underwater hover. Sometimes they played the game with Les not watching her mother throw the dime, but Ingrid said it made her nervous when Les stayed under the water so long, that she was afraid that it might hurt her brain.

Duke was sitting in a pool chair on the grass, smoking a cigar. He was fully dressed–he didn't have a bathing suit, he said. At least he'd taken off his good clothes. Still, he looked out of sorts, impatient and ill-at-ease, the beige banlon shirt too heavy, his green workpants a stiff armor, next to the flesh sprawled across the other chairs.

She dove down again and swam up between her mother's legs. Her mother's legs looked whiter, bonier, bigger, below the water, like the legs of a statue except for a few long hairs splaying to the sides.

Les didn't touch her mother's legs, but swam smack in-between, her face shooting straight up to the surface, hoping to be a surprise. Her mother did not react to her resurfacing, but stared towards the other side of the pool.

Les yanked her leg.

"You got it?" her mom said, holding out her hand for the dime.

Les gave it to her mother, then clasped her hand closed so she wouldn't throw it. "Mom," she asked. "How come Uncle Duke never goes swimming?"

Her mom sat back, pulling her legs up. "Gee, I don't know." She looked over at Duke, shading her eyes. "Maybe he doesn't know how."

"Doesn't know how to swim?"

"I don't know–don't think he had much of a chance to learn probably. Not when he was a kid."

"Oh Mom," Les said, incredulous. "Duke can do anything, you know that. I mean, he's the best golfer in the world, right? He's just got to know how to swim."

"Oh, he's a natural athlete." Ingrid turned the dime over in her palm. "And probably, if he was tossed into the sea, he'd figure out what to do. But I bet he's never actually learned. I didn't, till I was at University of Minnesota–it was a requirement, can you imagine that? You couldn't graduate without swimming. Grady went to Macallister and they didn't require it so she never did learn.... But Duke didn't go to school much, probably never did either unless it was in the Army, and, you know him, he was probably able to bluff his way around it by that time."

Les peeked over the side of the pool at him.

Something caught his attention and he gave her an exaggerated smile and wave. She smiled and waved back.

"You think he'd mind if I asked him."

"Sure, go ahead."

"Naw– I think it would really embarrass him."

Her mom turned back to her magazine. Les scooted under water, then slowly surfaced, bending her head back as she came up to smooth her hair back, to get it nice and slick. She thought it looked cool like that, made her face more grown up. When she put a towel over it, after swimming, it looked almost like a Mary, she always thought–one of the ones in those paintings.

Turning back towards the center of the pool, she jumped into a series of little dives.

She wondered if Duke watched her and tried to keep her legs straight, toes pointed. Like a dolphin, she thought, no, a mermaid better, no, one of those women that swam around old movies.

She pointed her toes harder than ever. Then it occurred to her that if he didn't know how to swim, her jumping around like that, pointing her toes so hard, might make him feel bad. She broke off her dives immediately, turning part way away, so it wasn't obvious that she was stopping on account of him. From the corner of one eye, she searched for his face.

But he wasn't even looking at her. He was standing up, feeling around his pockets with the palms of his hands (one holding a lit cigar), then walking somewhat stiffly toward her mom, bending down to her. He was pointing to his watch—her mom frowned up to the sun, shading her eyes with her hand, then nodded once, twice, and went back to the magazine. He straightened up and walked over towards the men's locker room.

Les pulled herself up out of the pool, gleaming wet, and followed him quickly, running flat-footed so she wouldn't stub her toe, but not too fast either, so the lifeguard wouldn't whistle.

When she reached him, she stopped abruptly, embarrassed in the soggy drip of her suit, to be next to him who was dressed, dry, had hair oil sculpting his hair, a cigar, and had probably never learned to swim. She folded her arms over her chest, pressed her legs closer together, squinted.

"What's up doll?"

"Are you leaving?"

"Yeah, well I have a couple of things to do. I thought I'd just go do them, then come back, pick you guys up–"

"Can I go with you?"

"Don't you want to stay here with your mom?"

"I won't come if you don't want me," she said.

"It's not that." He took her hand. His was like a bear paw, so warm and dry and big against hers, shrunken anyway with the hour in the water. "It's just, well, here your mom came to the pool and all–"

"She won't care."

He looked over at Ingrid, her legs propped up on the tiles at poolside, still bent over the magazine.

"Run and ask her," he said. "'Then hurry and get dressed. I can't wait around all day–"

Her heart swooped with joy. She ran so fast this time, the lifeguard blew his whistle at her–

Nodding wildly, she slowed to a scoot.

"Mom–" she called.

* * *

He waited for her out in the car. His waiting face was like her mother's waiting face, pre-occupied and slightly angry, but when he saw her, he took on a gleeful expression and rubbed his hands together like a cartoon villain plotting a dastardly deed. She laughed.

They drove quietly. She wanted to ask him where they were going but knew he didn't like questions. That was part of being a he-man, she decided; you didn't like answering questions.

"First, we go to the store," he said after a while.

The "store." The Lerners, the Catholic family with five children who lived next door called it that, and so did the Torellis, the Catholic family (with six children) across the street. But her own mom and dad were always very specific—"the grocery store", "the drug store", or even the actual store names—"Dart Drug", "the A&P", "Hechts". She had always thought that using the right names had something to do with her mother being a working mother, having a little more spending money than the bigger families next door.

After he pulled into the parking lot of their neighborhood shopping center, he took her hand and headed towards Murphy's. She'd only been there once before, with Carrie from next door. Murphy's just wasn't a store her parents went to. She and Carrie had bought fake fingernails with big pink half-moons that covered half her nails.

The light seemed dimmer than the stores she was used to, grayish to the point of pink. It reminded her of the light in an old black and white movie.

Duke kept hold of her hand and after asking the salesgirl, with a wink, about shaving cream and cigars, they went to those two aisles only. She only got a fleeting glimpse of a posterboard of artificial roses, pretend windows behind yellow net curtains, multicolored skeins of yarn, fans, styrofoam coolers, earrings and a shimmering of beads—but that was near where the fingernails had been, she remembered.

He walked fast, decided quickly.

The sky was blinding afterwards. As they squinted their way to the car, Duke noticed a sign at the Dart Drug next door for an instant winner lottery game.

"Christ, instant winner. I should have gone to that one," he said.

"It's just these little scratch-off things–"

"Oh yeah?"

"You know, like apples, pineapples–"

"Yeah?"

He redirected her across the parking lot with two hands pushing gently at her back, putt putt putt. His hands were so large, like he could scoop her right up. She laughed.

The Dart Drug was a bright store, green with black and white checks. It was supposed to look like a racing flag—"Your Automotive Center" one wall read.

There was a line at the check-out. Les hated waiting. If it were her dad, she would have said, 'come on, it's stupid; you know you'll never win.'

Duke looked down at her, squeezed her hand. She wished suddenly that he would buy something for her. Anything. She felt stupid wanting something, but she just did, some sign of something.

He had just about finished paying.

"Hey," he said, looking down at the change the sales girl placed into his large brown palm, and the ticket too–only he put the ticket in his breast pocket—"you want some...um...candy?" He turned to the stand behind them.

"You still like that kind of stuff, don't you? Hell," he winked at the sales girl, "I still like that kind of stuff–"

The sales girl laughed. Les too.

"So, what'll it be?"

Now, that he was buying something, she felt embarrassed. In a flustered blur, she picked out a tootsie roll pop, the first tried and true thing that came to hand.

"That's what you want?" he said. "You're sure?" He looked into her face seriously.

Was it awfully babyish?

She wished instantly that she could put it back, but she did not want the choice to seem important enough to put back.

"I guess so," she said.

He twirled the pop between his thumb and forefinger like a puny little baby's rattle. She felt her face reddening.

"Make that two," he nodded to the sales girl. Handing the tootsie roll pop back to Les, he squatted down next to her, whiskers touching her cheek, and faced the rows of candy–

"So, what color you get again?" he asked picking up the hand, hers, which now held the pop–

"Red, huh? Is red the best color?"

His blue eyes so wide and close, he was making fun of her–

But he seemed to read that thought too. "No, serious," he said. "If I'm going to try one of these things I want your favorite. 'Cause your favorite's the best huh?"

"Duke!"

"What's red anyway? Cherry, right? Or strawberry?"

"Cherry."

"Hmmm." He studied the pop between her fingers, turning her hand back and forth to read the label. The words were printed in white on colored paper, with tiny little drawings–

When he held her hand like that it reminded her of playing baseball together, the way he held her bat with her, showing her how to get a hit, making sure she did get a hit, hooting when Arne complained–

"This is the kind with the chocolate in the center right?"

She nodded.

He picked out another cherry, then stood, and taking her hand, they headed out of the store.

"After you, madame," he grinned, holding open the door.

Before he took her hand again, he unwrapped the tootsie roll pop and stuck it into his cheek, then he looked carefully, grandly, to his sides for oncoming traffic.

She skipped across the parking lot next to him. When they got to the car, he grinned down to her, his teeth huge around the little white stick.

"Cheers," he said, pulling out the red pop and raising it towards her with a nod.

Karin Gustafson

Was she supposed to say cheers too? She laughed and fingered the end of her pop, still keeping it in her mouth.

She thought they would go back to the pool for her mom and Arne, but Duke drove in the opposite direction.

As he drove, the tootsie roll pops were less of a joke. He kept his in his mouth as matter-of-factly as a cigarette. He kept it in even when he stopped at a Seven-Eleven, went inside, and came out with a six-pack. It was only after he tore the first beer away from the cardboard that he took the pop out.

It was just about all chocolate now. She thought his eyes looked over the gnawed lollipop with an expression of "yech," but he didn't say anything, just tossed it into the trash can next to the exit drive and pulling open the can of beer, took a sip.

She worried about the beer. Instead of heading back for the pool, he turned onto the highway.

As the landscape around the highway flattened, the inside of Duke's car seemed to grow. It was one of those nice squishy cars, gold inside. Her feet could hardly touch the floor the way he had the seat pushed back. From the rear-view mirror hung a small glass globe part-filled with pink liquid and decorated by a gold tassel. The pink must be some kind of perfume, she thought. A strong flowery scent wafted from the globe as it swung back and forth, doing battle with the lingering clouds of cigar and general man smell.

A lot of other air too at seventy-five miles an hour. She leaned against the window, trying to direct her head so that the wind would push the hair away from her forehead and not over it.

She liked the idea of her hair back and windblown. It reminded her of the way women looked in commercials. There was one of a woman who ran and ran, in slow motion, into the arms of a man who also ran. Because of the slow motion, they both looked like they were hopping instead of running and the woman's hair curled away from her head in a variety of lazy s's.

Her own hair was straight when the wind blew, straight when it was still. But how would it be if she ran like that, she wondered, in slow motion?

Duke turned off the highway and slowed the car into a small gravel road. It was down by the river, a place where people could park.

Duke pulled the car up to one of the big square logs marking a parking place, turned off the ignition, and without speaking or even waiting for the engine to fully swallow its purr, jumped out.

She sat there, listening to the ticking of the engine.

What did he want her to do?

She didn't worry about such things with her parents. But Duke always seemed to have something particular in mind, something he expected.

She undid her seat buckle slowly, cracked open the heavy door and awkwardly wedged herself out, her father's habitual 'watch your fingers' echoing in her head.

Duke stood several yards away where a bit of grass began, looking out at the river.

"See that, doll," he said, reaching his arm back for her. "A little sail boat.... Wow."

"Cool," she said.

"Boy," he said. "Must be nice out there, a day like today." He let his arm loosen and slide down her side so that his hand encompassed her hip.

"I used to dream of having a little sailboat like that," he said.

"You still might."

"Nah, not now, I'm too old now. I'm an old man." He laughed. Took a sip of his beer. "Not unless I win the lottery anyhow. Hey, what about that game?" He took his hand from her side and fished into his pocket for the ticket. "Let's see. You want to be the lucky scratcher." He went into another pocket for a coin and handed them both over.

She looked for a flat place to put the ticket down while she scratched it.

"Here, use my hand," he said, holding his thick palm flat.

One pineapple, two pineapples, three–a little red cherry.

"Shucks, no sail boat today," he groaned.

"Nobody ever wins at that game," she said, "except fifty cents."

"Fifty cents, ah, the cheapskates–"

"Yeah."

Nudging the gravel with the tips of his shoes he started down towards the river. She ran ahead of him, all the way to the blackened beams that lay at the bank. She stepped onto them carefully, arms out to her sides.

"Watch out there," he called, "I'm too old to go diving in there after you,"

She laughed back, picking up speed along the beam. She felt like a dancer with him watching her. "You're not so old," she shouted.

"Oh no," he said, coming down to her with an exaggerated huff, his hand upon his heart, "you don't think so–"

Then they were both quiet, Duke looking out to the water, Les waiting for whatever would come next.

"We better get back to your mom," he said. They turned to the car. Just then a big red Impala drove up right near the shore, stopping in a spray of gravel. The car was filled with colored people, a family.

A young very black man in plaid shorts got out first, nodding at Les and Duke. Then he went to the trunk for a bucket and fishing poles. Then came a couple of grown women, and tugging at each other to try to scramble out first, were four children.

One of the women was also very dark, her white sleeveless shirt vibrating against the mahogany of her upper arms where she held a baby in a pink lace dress and bonnet. The other woman was rounder and lighter with freckles. Whose kids, Les wondered? Which woman's? She liked to try to understand things like that, to make a story out of the things she saw. And what about the man?

One of the boys, in torn khaki shorts, went round to help with the buckets. The others whooped and jumped their way to the river beams. The lighter woman shouted after them to stop it, now, just hold on.

"Will you look at that?" Duke muttered as he quickened his pace for the car. "God damned blackies."

Les knew that Duke didn't really like colored people. Still, she was taken aback by the venom.

"Take over the old damn place if they could," Duke said. "Just see 'em, trying to now."

Les got in the car slowly. The flowery essence seemed a sick smell now, mixed with the traces of beer.

"God damned blackies–send 'em all back that'd be the best thing."

"You shouldn't say that, you know."

"What, send them back to Africa? What's so bad about that? Lincoln himself thought it was a good idea. What's that country, begins with an L?"

"No," she said, quietly. "I mean, that name."

He thought a second. "Blackies? That's what they all want now, right? Not colored, not negro–isn't that it?"

She wished he would just stop.

He settled and re-settled himself in the driver's seat, made as if to start the car, wiped his hands through his hair. "Christ," he said.

"It's just, well," she tried, "you shouldn't talk out loud like that. You want to hurt someone's feelings? Like those kids–you're not against little kids, are you?"

He looked down at her. His face seemed to visibly gentle, the skin smoothing, eyes rounding, even his oiled-back hair seemed to soften. He leaned back against the seat, trying, she could see, to be the essence of reason.

"Look, sugar," he said. "I don't want to hurt anyone, least of all little kids. I just think people should work for what they get. And a lot of colored people, blacks, whatever you want to call them—well, I just don't think they agree with that."

"That's not true. You know that's not true. A lot of...colored people...they work all the time. Mr. Thompson in the school and Daisy, you know, who used to help Mom, all kinds of people. Anyway, children can't go to work."

He rubbed his chin. "Oh sweetie, you give things to people they get so they just don't appreciate it. Look, how they just burned up all those stores and shit."

"But Uncle Duke. You don't know if those people out there get anything. You don't know if they burned anything either. And people were so upset after Martin Luther King was shot. Maybe they were wrong, but still, well...."

"I mean, just think how it would be, if you were poor and people were mean to you and you saw all these other people having all this stuff. I think that might make you really mad."

"Honey, I *was* poor," he said. "And people *were* mean to me. And I knew what I had to do, I had to go out and work, that's what. Make some money of my own. Get the hell out of there." He paused. "At least for a while."

"But it was different back then, wasn't it? Back in the Depression. I mean, I don't know for sure, but wasn't everyone poor?"

"Not everyone."

"But a lot of people, right? And today, just think of it, if you looked around and if all your stuff was bad and everyone else's looked so good, and then on top of that, people were treating you bad too, just because you were poor, or you know," she whispered, "colored."

"It sounds silly," she blushed, "but I think of it sort of like a dog. You know, if you're mean and you don't ever give it any love, it gets mean too, tries to bite just anyone. But if people are nice to the dog and pat it and give it good things to eat, then it will always be good too, it wouldn't even know how to bite–"

She stopped. He was smiling at her in that sly way he had.

"So you think all those people out there, those marchers, are like dogs, is that it? And what we really need to do," he smiled more broadly—"is throw them all about a half a dozen bones–Say 'here boy.'" He gestured to the group on the shore, whistling softly.

"Uncle Duke, stop it. Stop it right now. You know that's not what I mean."

"But I kind of like that idea. Here boy," he said, whistling again.

"Stop it."

He laughed, taking her hand. She tried to pull it away, but he wouldn't let her. She tried not to look at him too, but his eyes were dark shells aimed straight into her own and the seat was too narrow to turn away in.

"I'm sorry, sweetie," he said, "but that's such a lot of grownup talk."

"It's not like dogs, you know I didn't mean that—you know I didn't mean that about people."

"I know, honey pie."

"Can't we just go back now?"

He made no motion to start the car.

She looked at the kids playing, their dark skin solid against the glimmering river, a separate shine. A little black girl balanced on the beams by the shore but the other kids gathered around a bucket, jostling shoulders. One of the women was shouting at them, but they didn't seem to mind.

She thought about how unfair he was, Duke–how could he be so unfair?

Because he must not understand, she thought. Because somehow he must just not understand how people are, human beings. And she thought of this past spring too, and Martin Luther King Jr. dead in the night, and the crying and the sadness and the riots just down town, the smell of smoke they drove through even weeks later, stores with boards nailed up, big X's marking the grain.

The sailboat was closer now, the red and white stripes as bright as a toothpaste tube. But it did look nice out there, she thought, the trees across blurring like trees in a painting, soft feathery brush-stroked trees.

"Look, I'm sorry," Duke said. "Here you are talking all this stuff, really just incredible for a kid your age, and me playing the fool–"

"It's just that..." she tried.

"What?"

"No."

"Come on. Look, I really am sorry, sweetie." His eyes drooped as sorrowfully as a hound.

She sighed. "It's just, well, you know how you always hear people talking about good people and bad people. You know like people that do crimes and stuff being bad. Countries too. You know how Grandma always says that about the Germans or the Russians, what mean people she thinks they are."

She winced.

He nodded.

"It sounds sort of stupid, but I guess what I believe is that there really isn't such a thing as good people or bad people, any of that stuff. What I think is that all people are really good, deep down at least, and if they're treated well and people love them– not that having stuff is so important, a nice house and everything–but you know, if they don't feel like the whole world's forgotten them or better than them, well, then I think they'll grow up to be good. But if they're treated really mean, and they always have everything bad and mad and awful, then, well, I think that then they'll grow up to be angry. And how can you blame them? I mean, of course if they do something really bad, you know kill someone, that's terrible, but when it's like no one's even cared—"

Duke was quiet. Then, "that sounds pretty good," he said slowly, face and voice grave. "But where does that leave me, huh? When are people going to start being nice to me?"

Stretching, his chest curled like a bear's, he reached his arms toward her, growling and gnashing his teeth.

She wanted to be mad, she was mad, but she also began to laugh as he took her over easily, pulling her next to him.

"Huh?" he said, "so what about me, huh?"

"Duke!" she said. "Stop it," laughing. "let go."

* * *

How strange it was, she thought as they drove back, to find out what people believed. Duke was wrong. She'd have to help him somehow, persuade him.

But a lot of people were like that. She remembered how shocked she was when they started having current events in school and she found out how many kids in her class, kids that she thought of as cool kids, even sort of friends, were for the war, and that they were against colored people too, though they didn't usually say that directly. Usually, they just went on against the marchers.

It was the boys mainly; the girls, other than Les, didn't talk much about that stuff.

How stupid it was for the U.S. to fight with one hand tied behind its back. How the protesters were stupid hippies, only wanting to take drugs.

That people should just work harder if things were so bad.

And then, even with the air blowing in on her face, and she remembered that day in the conference room, the game of hangman, the words she'd flubbed, and how those same boys acted like she was such an idiot, like she knew nothing, and she felt hot and made and glad she wouldn't have to see them, hardly any of them, the whole summer long, the cool kids living mainly in a whole different part of her neighborhood, the new part.

When she and Duke got back to the base, they had to show her card to get in. The soldiers were very young this time, the white one so closely shaved his skin looked like a young piglet's, the black guard's skin not raw but awfully shiny.

After she showed them the card, they saluted her. She felt her own face turning red, waiting for them to laugh, but they didn't, their eyes didn't even flicker.

Duke didn't salute back this time. "The creeps," he said, shoving his beer can down by the gas pedal.

He was worried about her mom and Arne, she thought. They'd been away too long.

But her mom and Arne were already gone when they got there.

"Oh-oh," Duke said. "Looks like we blew it."

They drove back to her house fast, Duke muttering between sips of a beer. "We're in for it now."

She felt her heart crawling up her throat. But when they got home, it all turned out fine. Mrs. Wainwright, a friend of her mom's, and her son Jeff, a friend of Arne's, had given them a ride home, and were there still, staying for dinner.

Les could tell from the way Arne groaned as Duke apologized, that Ingrid *had* been mad. But now she was talking with Mrs. Wainwright, who had gone to art school, about how the color combinations had worked out in the living room. ("A little dark, yes, but so elegant," Mrs. Wainwright said. Ingrid beamed.)

At Mrs. Wainwright's suggestion, Ingrid was making hot dogs with cheese whizz in the middle. Mrs. Wainwright was always one for not making a fuss. She worked too, so she knew what it was like, she said.

"Stupid bitch," Les heard Duke grumble as he went downstairs to wash up. He didn't like Mrs. Wainwright. Because she was a widow, Les thought, and kind of chubby, and so, teary in the way of a widow, jolly in the way of a chubby person. Both things seemed to get on Duke's nerves.

But Les thought it was nice to have people to supper. They didn't have people much unless it was planned, and when it was planned, it was always a big deal.

She went to help in the kitchen though her mom was hard to help, especially when they had guests. Usually Les just had to stand around watching her mom work nervously and then slip in and do something that her mom might not notice or wasn't getting to or would finally allow.

But it was different with Mrs. Wainwright there. Mrs. Wainwright was the kind of person who just barged ahead and did stuff, who didn't pay attention to her mom's hints about the way she liked things done.

The unrestrained help made her mom nervous, Les could tell.

"I hope it's okay," she kept saying. She had opened a bottle of wine they had laying around. They didn't drink wine usually. This was an old Christmas present from someone at her dad's lab.

The wine was called Sangria. It had a filigreed S that curved over the label, engraved over a charging bull.

"It'll be great," Mrs. Wainwright said. "Spanish wine is my favorite."

As Ingrid took a sip, her face crinkled. "Eeeuw. I should have known. The people at that lab, I tell you. Here, what do you think?" She offered the glass to Mrs. Wainwright. "Too sour, huh?"

"I think it's okay," Mrs. Wainwright said, pressing her lips together.

"But don't you think it's awfully sour?" Ingrid said doubtfully. "What do you think?" she turned to Les.

"Me?"

"Just a sip."

Les dutifully sipped, all the time thinking "wine" excitedly.

"Yeech."

"Here, I'll fix it," Mrs. Wainwright said.

She poured the bottle out into a big pitcher. Les could feel her mother's alarm. Then she began adding orange juice, lemonade, orange slices, ice cubes.

"Don't water it down too much," Ingrid said. "Wait a sec. Here, maybe I should do it. You think I should just do it?"

Mrs. Wainwright laughed. "Just go chop your cabbage."

Les smiled.

"And how are you my Daisy Darling?" Mrs. Wainwright asked whenever she walked past her, touching or smoothing her hair. Les thought she must like blonde hair. Hers was stiffly bleached.

Her mom chopped with frowning intensity.

"You honestly think hot dogs are okay? You know they're really not my style."

"They're great, great. Look, tell your cousin it was my idea. Blame it on me," Mrs. Wainwright laughed.

Ingrid groaned.

"At least they *smell* good," Les said.

The boys went outside with paper plates and a chessboard. Les stayed in with the grown-ups.

The sangria seemed to make Duke like Mrs. Wainwright better.

"So you made this stuff?" he asked.

Mrs. Wainwright nodded.

"Grew the grapes and everthing?"

Mrs. Wainwright giggled, round cheeks pink.

"It's good, isn't it?" Les said.

"'It's good, isn't it?'" Duke mimicked. "How do you know?

"But it *is* good," Ingrid said. "You should have tasted that old wine before Ellen fixed it up." She stuck out her tongue in distaste. "You want some ice?" She spooned some out of the pitcher. "It needs more ice, doesn't it?"

Mrs. Wainwright and Duke ate heartily. Her mom sat back and drank. Though she had alcohol rarely, she liked to drink it when she had it and not eat much. She hated, she said, 'to spoil the effect.'

Mrs. Wainwright, like Duke, was a big Republican. She hated LBJ, JFK (though she always insisted she was sorry for Jackie), and thought anybody who went to Sweden should be put in prison. She was also really afraid of the colored people that lived up on Saint Barnabas road.

"I tell you, it's even getting bad out there," Duke was saying. "Out in Minnesota, and believe me, there's not a black face in sight–too damn cold for 'em."

Les groaned inside. Mrs. Wainwright chuckled.

"I tell you, it's like a poison we got going on in this country, the whole thing–" Duke went on.

He was going to talk about the farm next, Les thought, her grandmother's old farmhouse.

Sure enough.

"Did Ing tell you what happened to the old farmhouse out there?" Duke leaned into the table to focus his energy upon Mrs. Wainwright.

Ingrid who had been taking spoonfuls of Sangria all this while, now took a full symbolic sip. "Oh come on Duke," she said then. "I can't hear about all that now, it just makes me too sick."

But of course, she did want to hear about the farmhouse, Les thought, because the next minute, she started talking about it herself–

"You know my mom's farm?" she said turning to Mrs. Wainwright. "I told you, didn't I?"

Mrs. Wainwright shook her head, no.

"It's not the farm exactly, the house. Didn't I tell you?"

Mrs. Wainwright shook her head one more time, said, "no, you didn't tell me."

The story, which Ingrid told at length now, was how the kids, they thought it was kids anyway, local teenagers, had wrecked it up, tore it all apart, broken windows, scrawled all over the walls—"It was this spring, I haven't even seen it yet, but if it's like they say–"

"I've seen it," Duke jumped in, "and, my land, did they do a number on it. Incredible! Tore the toilet out of the bathroom and sat it down in the living room, even took a you-know-what out there, right there in the middle of the floor." He whistled, shook his head.

Her mom wrinkled up her nose as if actually smelling the you-know-what right then and there. Mrs. Wainwright made a face of absolute wonder.

"Stripped the wallpaper, even the plaster, punched right damn through the walls. And these are white kids I'm talking about, 'less they imported some colored ones up from Chicago for the night–"

"It wasn't a fancy house. It wasn't all fixed up," Ingrid said, "but it was nice–a nice decent little house. Why, they re-did it all before they moved into town, the wallpaper, the walls, new fixtures and everything. Seemed such a shame when they moved."

Les quietly eyed a curly-q of cheese whizz on her plate. She could hardly remember that house, though she knew she had visited it–they had gone out to get eggs from the renter. What she remembered was that it was pretty broken up even then, a hole in the floor by the stairwell that a big mouse, maybe even a rat, ran out of. The boy living there, the renter's son, made a game of trying to catch it, a show to scare her. A little boy with a big hat, scrambling around the floor right next to that mouse, rat, getting it into the corner. A bare electric bulb burning overhead, still the whole place seemed dark–

"I told Mom they should always make the renter live in the house, but they just wanted the fields–that's how they are out there now, just wanting more land to grow soybeans. So with no one there keeping track of it..." Ingrid shrugged, stared grimly at the center of the table.

Les hated it when her mom got like that.

Duke smiled, reached for the sangria, offered some to Mrs. Wainwright who said, "why not?" then to Ingrid who in the inner space of the ruined farm house didn't respond. He shrugged and finished the bottle in his own glass.

"Yeah, I'll tell you..." he started. But then he sipped his wine, not going on.

What were Arne and Jeff up to, Les wondered.

"Miss, uh miss," Duke said then, his voice lightening.

Les looked up.

He winked.

"So, they got any spare coffee in this joint?"

Les' face tried to signal 'not now'.

"You're on duty right? Well, if you don't mind, I'd like a cup of coffee, please. And make that with cream and sugar, sugar."

She stormed out to the kitchen.

"Ahem," he cleared his throat. "And oh, Miss, do you mind clearing the table?"

Cheeks burning, she came back and got his plate.

"Say, when do you get off nights, doll? 'Cause you know I'm free later.

"I'm happy to stay late if you want," he said when she came back for the other plates. "I got all the time in the world for a girl like you."

Mrs. Wainwright watched them intently, her round cheeks nudged into a slightly confused smile. Her mom seemed oblivious, still preoccupied by the farm.

"By the way, you ain't married are you?" Duke asked.

"Would you like some coffee?" Les asked Mrs. Wainwright, trying to ignore him.

"Sure, sweetie–you need some help?"

"No, I can do it."

"Mom, you want coffee?"

Her mother sighed. "Sure, Les, I guess so. Kind a' hate to lose the effect of this nice wine."

"Then don't," Mrs. Wainwright said. "Enjoy."

Les put all the dishes by the sink. It was getting to be sunset outside. She stood on tiptoe to look down at the boys on the back patio. She couldn't actually see them, but she knew how they would be, hunched over the chess board, not noticing that it was too dark to play until it was practically black out. Boys seemed to be like that, to be allowed to be like that, to skip. While girls had to be nice all the time. At least pretty girls did. If people thought you were pretty, then you had do what they wanted, be nice. It was like you owed it to them.

"Look at that," Duke said, when she came back with the cups, the saucers, the pitcher, the little sugar bowl. "How nice." He pinched her cheek. "And how nice," he said, this time with a leer, eyeing her up and down.

"Thank you, Daisy," Mrs. Wainwright said. "You know I call her my Daisy Darling."

Les flushed darker.

Her mom took another sip of wine, her glass still half-full.

"Now, Les," Duke said.

Good, she thought. He seemed to have left the restaurant game.

"Sit down here a second, I have a question for you. First, you want anything? Not coffee, I know that, but dessert. Ice cream or something?"

Her mom sighed. "You want some ice cream, Duke?"

"Not me, I'm not an ice cream kind of guy, you know that, Ing."

"You, Ellen? It's that good kind."

Mrs. Wainwright paused, her round face swelling with the wish. "Maybe a little…"

Les started to get up for it, but Duke took her hand, keeping her at her place—"No just wait here a second, Les, her dessert can wait a minute. Can you wait a minute on the dessert?" he said, turning to Mrs. Wainwright. "You're not going to waste away, right? 'Cause this here is important now."

'Important now–' Les hated the sound of that. She tried to look sympathetically at Mrs. Wainwright, whose face had immediately flushed with the words 'waste away'.

"Now, Les, now tell me, okay. I have a question for you. I mean this is really between me and you, Les," he lowered his voice, "but these other two are here. You don't mind, do you?"

As he bent down to whisper to her, she smelled the wine on his breath, a sour fruity smell that brought to mind the filigreed S on the bottle, the charging bull. A scent of beer next to his neck.

She shook her head, yes, yes she did mind.

He didn't seem to notice.

"Okay, so I was thinking about what you were talking about to me earlier, what we were talking about," he wiped his face. "So let's take those boys out in Minnesota—that's what I was thinking about, you got me? Now tell me what bad thing happened to them to make them go beat down Grandma's farmhouse? What do you think, out there with all that fresh air, green grass? Remember, we're not talking city now.

We're not talking Harlem or Detroit here. Nope, we're talking about a pretty damn good life."

He leaned back, crossing his arms, waiting for her to respond.

She tried to send some message that he should just stop, but his gaze was taken over by something that blanked her out.

"I don't know," she said.

"Hmmm. You don't know, right? You don't know. But really now, why should you know? A girl like you couldn't even think of those crap things." He cleared his throat, looking defiantly at her mom and Mrs. Wainwright.

"But I know," he said, sitting back in his chair. "Maybe from my own wild days." He smiled. "I *do* know what bad thing happened to them to make them turn so sour.... And you know what it was?"

He turned back to Les, acting once more like he was only talking to her.

"I'll tell you what it was. Nothing. Nothing bad happened to them. They were given all this good stuff, just like most people in this damn Great Society these days–we're not talking Depression now–and you know what they did with it? You know what they did with it?"

Mrs. Wainwright, on the opposite side of the table, was breathless with anticipation.

"Duke–be careful," her mother said.

"Just ran it into the ground, that's what." He snapped his fingers. "Poof. That's all there is to it. Let's go out and raise hell. That's what they *want* to do."

"You don't have to tell me," her mother said, again furious. But not at Duke, Les realized. It was those boys out in Minnesota.

Les wished she could just sink under the table, crawl out from around their legs.

"But I want to tell you," Duke said. "And I want to tell *you*," turning back to Les. "Because I've been thinking about that theory of yours," he chuckled. "Honestly–I've been mulling it over in this old noggin of mine.

"You know your daughter has a theory don't you?" he said to Ingrid. "About–what do you call it? What makes people tick? Uhhh, psychology, that's it–crime and punishment, raising children, war on poverty, you name it. An absolutely beautiful theory, you hear her talk, better than any of those old farts sitting up there in the Capitol–you ever heard her?"

Her mother shook her head. Les reddened.

"My land, you should listen sometime. Boy, can that girl talk about this stuff. It takes your breath away."

Ingrid looked at Les, half-smiling. Les tried to shrug.

"But listen, listen to me now," he went on, "cause I've been thinking about all this. You may not believe it's possible, but I've been mulling it around this old noggin of mine, and I come up with a theory of my very own." His eyes grinned mischievously. "I call it the Uncle Duke Onion theory–what do you think? Maybe the Uncle Duke Human Onion Theory is better?"

He looked up to the group for the answer. Ingrid was silent. Mrs. Wainwright nodded eagerly. Les willed him to just shut up. Should she turn on the TV?

"So you want to hear it?" he asked again.

"Let's hear it," Ingrid said.

He smiled, sighed, rubbed his chin. "Well, Les' theory is that people are born good. Okay," he said, acknowledging Les' grimace, "not really. Actually none of this is going to be near so nice as she explained, I really won't do justice to it, but just bear with me a little." He looked down, scratched his head, paused, a parody of the thinker.

"Don't laugh," he said. "She didn't really say it this way, okay? This is just the way I thought it–I 'interpreted' it, right? That how you say it? That people are sort of like nuts... Let's say walnuts, sounds a little classier. Let's not," he whispered sotto voce, "say niggertoes."

As Duke seemed to expect, this brought an explosion of giggles from Mrs. Wainwright. He looked at her sternly, his professor self, and would not go on until she quieted.

"Okay," he said, clearing his throat. "The idea of it, I think, is that when life is hard for people growing up they get this real hard shell on the outside, all that meanness and everything turning them hard and mean too. But this is just on the outside, because, according to Les' theory, if you can just crack through that hard shell, then you can get to the good stuff, the nice soft nut inside." He smiled.

"Right?" he asked Les, "the good person inside, right? Isn't that sort of it?"

"No," she shook her head. "No, it isn't."

"Okay, but it's something like that, isn't it?"

"No."

"Okay, she don't like the way I say it, so maybe we should call that one the nut theory then, and not hook it on Les. Just the nut theory plain.

"But getting onto my theory, the Uncle Duke theory–"

In a second, his face changed, the beaming smile graying, even his chin seeming to bristle with the whiskers of an older, world-weary, man.

"And this is important now, Les. You can learn something from this. Now in my theory, the Uncle Duke theory, I don't think of people as being like nuts. No, *I* think they're more like onions...." He paused.

"You know how an onion is, right? It has that thin brown peel on the outside and it's sort of hard there too. And inside there's all those different layers."

"Okay," Mrs. Wainwright said.

"Now in Les' theory, I mean, ahem, the nut theory, you think you can somehow peel off people's outer shells, all that meanness, and come to something completely different inside–the good nut, right? But just think of an onion. You can try peeling it, being nice and all, but just think about it. Have you ever peeled an onion? Every time you take off a layer, what do you find?" As he spoke, he rolled an invisible onion between his hands, manipulating the imagined weight with such conviction that the women were drawn to the thick puffed flesh of his palms, his heavy but graceful fingers and the ringed core they seemed to carry. "More onion, right? Then you peel again," he peeled. "More onion." He smiled. "And again, right? And again. In fact, no matter how much you peel away," and now he flattened his hands, letting the whole thing drop away—"that's what you're left with. More rotten stinking onion, all the way down to the end, the same rotten stinking onion through and through."

Les felt like he'd thrown her across the room.

Her mom's face lips pressed tightly together.

Mrs. Wainwright's lips were tight together too, but her face and eyes and cheeks were round, shining, as if suppressing a cheer that the silence didn't yet allow.

Duke sat back in his chair.

"But ain't it the truth?" he said at last, addressing himself now only to his distant cousin. "Ain't it just the truth, Ing?"

Les' mom looked grimly at the dregs of her sangria. "I don't know if it's as bad as all that," she said.

"Oh no! Sure it is. Come on, Ing, be honest now. Look, it's for her own education."

"It certainly is an interesting way to think about things," Mrs. Wainwright said.

"Shit, don't give me that," Duke said.

"I just don't think it's that bad," Ingrid said.

Duke shook his head in irritated disbelief.

"Don't listen to them," he said, turning to Les. "They don't know a goddamn thing."

"Let me get that ice cream," Ingrid said, going out to the kitchen.

"Come on Ing, it's for her own protection. You got to protect a girl like that," he shouted after her.

Now he sighed and looked back to Les, his face changed again, converting to boyish and clean-shaven.

"Hey doll," he said, "you wouldn't mind getting your old Uncle Duke a little scoop?"

"You said you weren't the ice cream kind."

"But maybe I'm just a little bit the ice cream kind, a teensy weensy bit," he said. "Come on, sweets, for your old Uncle Duke."

Out in the kitchen, her mom had the carton out.

"Duke wants some too," Les said.

"I knew he would." She took down another small crystal bowl. "You want a little too, Hon?"

Looking at the crystal dish in his mother's wet, veined hands, some of Les' upset lifted. It felt good to have her mom doing the ice cream, to be with her mom while she prepared ice cream. Her mom didn't just scoop out ice cream; she sliced bananas on it, swirled chocolate sauce, all in little crystal bowls.

"Should we get some for the boys?" her mom asked. "Or just wait till they come up? Why don't we just wait? I don't want them taking these bowls out on the porch."

"Duke says he just wants a little one," Les said.

"He sure gets carried away, huh?"

Les felt her face flushing again.

Her mom folded the pink carton carefully, wiping a dishrag over the bump of ice cream that slid down the side. "You shouldn't take him too seriously, you know. He never can be completely sensible and then with the wine talking–"

"I know," Les said.

When she brought him his ice cream, Duke put his arm around her. "So now you know doll, huh?" he said, "You don't want any of these young boys, right, out raising hell?"

When he smiled, she smelled the beer. The beer talking she thought, correcting her mom.

"Naw." He smiled and pulled her closer, "take someone tried and true."

"Oh dear, she really is a daisy darling, isn't she?" Mrs. Wainwright said dreamily.

"Don't give her that shit," Duke said, slamming his hand upon the table. "She's herself, that's what she is. She doesn't need no daisies, Jesus Christ."

Mrs. Wainwright jumped back in her chair, her face white, mouth clamped shut. Les felt a little sorry for her, but also glad. She never did like that name.

"I'm sorry," Duke said, "but just let the girl be herself."

"I wasn't trying to make her be anything else at all," Mrs. Wainwright sniffed.

"Nah, this girl, she don't need no daisy darlings, any of you guys. This little girl, she knows more in her little finger, more about men, how to please a man, then you guys in your whole big rump."

"Duke," Ingrid warned.

"I'm serious, Ing. You two–well, all you women nowadays–oh Jesus."

He wiped his hands through his hair, then, as if coming up with a great idea, he smiled, turned back to Les, and slowly, carefully, took a cigar out of his pocket.

Les could feel her mother's tension rise like a sharp intake of breath. For all the morning resolutions, she didn't think her mom could take a cigar right now.

But, after unwrapping the cigar and peeling off its small red band, Duke just lay it down on the table. He took Les' hand and held it in the air.

"So, how about it?" he said, slipping the cigar band over her third finger, her ring finger. It was too big and hung crazily. "Uh-oh," he said, taking it off that finger and put it on the middle one. "There, that's better."

"She *is* an awfully good girl," her mother said.

* * *

The next day when Duke picked her and Arne up at the pool, her stomach hurt terribly.

It was because she had to go to the bathroom. No. 2. She didn't like to put these things in words, even in her own head, but that's what it was. She'd had to go all day on and off at the pool but she hated pool bathrooms, any public bathroom, but pool bathrooms especially what with all those wet spots on the floor around the toilet and even on the seat, puddles you were never quite sure of. She didn't pee at the pool if she could help it, so she certainly wasn't going to—

Holding it till she got home was something she was used to. But this time something had gone wrong. She had cramps in the car and by the time they got home she could hardly walk. Duke had parked the car in back as usual so there was that big side hill to climb to get in the front, to the upstairs bathroom.

Arne bounded ahead up the hill, but she followed Duke slowly to the back door and into the downstairs.

"You okay, doll?"

"Yeah," she said. Then grimacing at another cramp, "sort of."

"What's wrong? Your stomach? Here, you have to go to the bathroom?" he guessed in his easy way, then laughed and held open the door for her. "Go on, go on, don't let me stop you."

She turned painfully towards the stairs.

"Here, go on down here, doll," he said, "if it's all that bad."

She hurried ahead of him, around the corner and through the flimsy bathroom door, a new one, which she hurriedly shut.

A big whew just to peel down the slick pink nylon of her suit. Hurrah to sit down on a clean toilet. The darkish coolish silence of her own house enveloped her like a pillow, held her in that accumulated quiet a house seems to gather in hours left to itself. She sighed.

Now that she was sitting, the sense of urgency lifted almost immediately and she felt a little silly to have actually told Duke her problem. She hadn't really told him, but she had let him guess, rushing into his bathroom like that. His bathroom. She kind of hated to mark it too, to let him know that part of her, her bathroom smell.

She put her bare tan feet on the lavender bathtub in front of her. She could hear Duke whistling somewhere. She could hear Arne too vaguely, his big old feet walking around upstairs. And now, maybe–what was that?–Arne had turned on the TV.

She waited, pushed. It hurt enough, but nothing would come. Or maybe a little.

She pressed down hard on her thighs as she often saw her mother do. But this only seemed to make her bottom hurt more.

She pushed, pressed down. The stool felt like a knife. Tears started in surprise at the pain, squeezing out of the corners of her eyes.

It hurt so much now she couldn't even push. Stuck there. That's what it felt like. She imagined the oversized stool half hanging out of her.

Nothing like this had ever happened to her before. 'Nothing like this has ever happened to me before.' The phrase began playing like a mantra, a mantra of apology.

Stuck there, and Duke in the next room.

'Nothing like this has never happened to me before–that's what she wanted to call out to him. 'Honestly.'

'Never ever ever.'

'Nothing like this.'

Warm air wafted down from the narrow window overhead.

Sweat poured down her face, the coolness of the swimming pool evaporated.

What she had to try to do was just calm down.

She twisted around to look at Duke's toiletry bag and shaving stuff sitting behind her, on the top of the toilet. Next to them was a special cup Duke had with a woman in a bathing suit.

Arne had shown her this cup years ago in Minnesota. On the outside of the cup, the woman wore a bathing suit, but when you looked inside to drink, the same woman was standing there naked.

Les looked into the cup now. You could see the woman's bare ultra white breasts, little pink nipples, but she was standing so that her hands and legs carefully covered everything else. The woman an old-fashioned kind of woman, with curly blonde hair like a movie star from the forties, and a sly winking look.

Did she have hair down there, Les wondered? She turned the cup at angles to scrutinize it.

Her mother had hair. Les didn't. And this woman wouldn't either, she thought, if she were able to move her hands away.

She couldn't imagine Duke drinking out of the cup if the woman had hair, not even to brush his teeth.

Just as she was really enjoying thinking about all this, she was assailed by another round of cramps. She sat the cup down quickly, trying to quiet herself.

Duke's footsteps. "Hey, doll, you okay in there?" he called.

"Yeah," she tried.

"You sure?"

"Oh!" A sudden knife cut through her backside.

"You have some problem, doll?"

She swallowed. "I'm okay."

She heard him walk away.

She was going to try now even if it really hurt, she told herself. Just try to get it over with.

But it hurt too much.

"Les are you okay? What's wrong?"

"Duke." Tears slid down her face like something melting.

"What? What's wrong? You okay? You can tell your old Uncle Duke, honey."

"Duke," she said in an immense act of will, "it feels like it's stuck."

"Stuck, ooh boy." She thought she heard him laugh.

"Duke it hurts," she said, her voice angry, anguished and trying to laugh too, all at the same time.

"Okay doll, just a second, okay? Let me think a second, doll, let me just think"

"Oh–"

"Can I come in?" he asked.

Her cheeks were burning. It wasn't him seeing her naked so much as on the toilet

"I can't help you unless I come in," he said.

"Okay," she said.

The moment he opened the door, he filled the room. His body seemed to inhabit its own shadow, taking up twice its allotted space.

He opened up the medicine cabinet, fiddled around with bottles which he read, "Damn," put back. Then took up his toiletry kit.

He paid no mind to her at all. He seemed not to even see her.

Finally, he found what he was looking for–a small blue jar, unscrewed it and stuck it in her face. It was half full of small white sticks that looked like little candles.

"Here take one of these and stick it up your heinie," he said, looking directly at her for the first time.

Her ears turned bright red with that word–his typical word for bottom. Somehow it was different now that he was actually talking about her.

"You want me to do it?" he asked.

"No!"

Shutting the door gently, he went out again. She read the label on the jar–glycerin, beeswax, other words too long, then took out one of the small candles, pressing it tightly between her fingers so it wouldn't slip away.

She couldn't imagine putting anything at all down there, especially if she was in the middle of going to the bathroom.

Just holding it, a slippery little totem, she pressed on her legs in once last try. This time, under threat of suppository, her body gave way.

She felt absolute joy. She sprang up, amazed that her bottom hardly hurt at all now, amazed it could recover so quickly, just like that, debated what to do about the slippery waxy thing, rolled it up in toilet paper, flushed it away, washed her hands of the remnants, and pulling her bathing suit up over that miraculously recovered bottom but not bothering in her sweaty relief to pull it all the way up over her shoulders, she danced out into Duke's room.

They called this room the "backroom" because it was farthest from the downstairs door. It was not a true basement room, only partly below ground. The other end had windows that peeked over the back lawn.

She jumped onto Duke's bed giggling and sat with her knees up.

"So, what do you think of the wall?" he asked.

He had put up a side of wood paneling to make a closet.

"So, what do you think of my toes?" she responded, laughing and wiggling them.

"Pretty classy, huh?" he said, looking back towards the smooth fake finish.

"So, what do you think of my knees?" she mocked, pulling them up to her chest and hugging them.

He looked over at her.

"So, what do you think of my stomach?' she said, still laughing. She stood up on the bed, hands on the bare skin of her waist and circled her tummy around as if it were a hula-hoop.

He pushed out his cigar into a heavy blue ash tray Arne had made in kindergarten, then was next to her in a second. His hands were warm and heavy against her as he picked her up, put her first on his knee and then stood her down on the floor. The white linoleum felt icy against the soles of her feet, his hands were so warm, huge upon her chest and back and rib cage.

She knew immediately that something was wrong. Was he mad at her for standing on his bed? Flattening his palm against her equally flat chest and finding her nipple, he squeezed it between his thumb and forefinger. She froze. What was it? Why was he doing that?

He knelt down before her pressing his warm coarse face against her bare stomach. At the same time, he pulled her bathing suit down over her legs. She lifted her feet one at a time and he wriggled the leg holes over them.

Her skin where the bathing suit had been felt cold and moist, like the underbelly of a fish, not used to air, light.

The skin of his neck looked dry, brown, deep straight lines at the back and on the side etched in crisscross. He moved away from her for a moment to shut the back room door.

As he put a finger from one hand inside her, she found herself focusing on the fingers of the other hand, his free hand. She was actually holding onto the arm of that hand for support. In fact from that side of her body, it looked rather like he was helping her to balance herself, to stand, like she was putting her shoes on.

The fingers on the free hand, the support hand, were very big. This is what struck her first and perhaps why it was hurting her so much down where the other fingers worked. She remembered falling hard against the bar of Arne's green bike once, how it hurt right there.

But this was different. Not like in the bathroom either. It hurt in her hips, her bottom—what she called that place was her front. It was like being choked down there, someone's hands around your neck, not your neck.

"Just take it easy," he said.

She pretended not to hear him. She pretended that nothing was happening.

"Sssshhh," he said.

It seemed to be something she had to get right. Long black hairs sprouted over the fingertips of his free hand like hair on a doll, each follicle distinctly separate. She looked at these small holes intently, tracing the particular hair that curled away from each one. The hand below stopped pushing now.

His whole body trembled. She could feel it through his clothes. The house creaked, stuttered.

Get out of here; get away.

Was her mother home?

Get this thing out of me.

The smell of cigars was overpowering. She hadn't noticed it at first, not once the fingering had begun. But now it reasserted itself powerfully, as if a white cardboard Dutch Masters box had enclosed her. Open wide, snap shut and the cellophane wrapper tightened around her, sausage roll, and the red paper wedding ring open wide snap shut

Middle finger. It meant fuck, Arne had told her. Her cousin too. That was a word they never said, only spelled. The f-word.

It was over. He moved away, turned broad back, green shirt, baggy chino pants. She unraveled her bathing suit from the floor and put it on quickly so he wouldn't see. He wasn't looking.

She looked up at his back. She could see or thought she could, that he was taking a handkerchief from his pocket, wiping his hands on it, then passing the same handkerchief over his face. It was a movement that surprised and somewhat disgusted her, how he could touch his face with that same cloth.

He stayed turned away from her, the handkerchief up to his face again and again.

It was a long time before she realized he was crying. She focused instead on how he could wipe his face with a handkerchief that had touched a finger that had been inside her, the place where she peed.

His crying sounded like a snuffling of water, a broken pipe in a ditch. It was different from her Dad's–a bird's coo. She had heard her Dad only once, when her dog had died.

She crossed her legs and looked down. White tile over gray cement, the floor always cool there, dank ice of cement leaching through. When she and Arne and their friends played war or tag or hide and go seek and got really sweaty they would pull up their shirts and lie chest down on it.

She spread out her hips, crossing her legs still, but allowing that part of her, her bottom–no it was really her front–to press against the tile.

It was very cool and hard and it took her away from him. Leaning more deeply forward, she flattened her torso onto the tile. She lay her head on its side away from him.

He sniffed, turning towards her.

"You know, Les," he said quietly.

"Sweetie, I'm sorry," he burst out.

She kept her eyes down.

He sniffed. In her mind, his face was angry. She didn't know how she saw it, because she didn't look directly at him but at some refraction of him that jittered across the floor.

"I hope you're not planning to tell your mom about this," he said.

*   *   *

When she was younger, she had been afraid at night. Every night at what she imagined was the stroke of twelve, she awoke to find a man coming out of her closet. She would call her father who would trudge into the hallway, say "it's okay," and shepherd her into her parents' room where she ran into her mother's bed.

She had realized examining the closet when the lights were on, that the man was probably the trunk of the upright vacuum, draped by clothes. But even knowing that, the imaginary clock still woke her at the imagined twelve, the man still stepped out, and she still called out for her father, who hardly woke up after a while, but still managed to stumble to into the hall by her door so she could run to the safety of her mother's sleep-soft back.

She hadn't woken up like this for some time, but now she was afraid again. She wished her father were home. She wished she could just sleep with her mom.

She asked her if she could sleep in her father's bed since he was gone. Her mom thought it was the air conditioning she wanted and said, sure.

Les was relieved at first. But when she snuggled into the deep hollow in the center of her dad's mattress, she found she could hardly breathe for the smell of the old pajamas he stuffed in a corner of the closet just behind the bed post, and coming from the closet itself, the scent of black shoe leather, sweat, old ties, woolen trousers not aired for several months.

Too much man. And the sheets and pillows were frosted with small bumps, the curdle of overwashed fabric. It was like her father to pick out sheets like that for his bed, the oldest cruddiest ones, saving the good ones in some ridiculous attempt to please her mom.

Despite her agitation, she held herself still until her mom slept, then moved into her bed.

Ingrid didn't seem to notice. She was pretty used to Les slipping in beside her.

A part of her wanted to press up against her mother, right into that outer silk of pink flannel nightgown, worn so smooth over her mom's hips that it was barely a layer above the dimpled thighs and the harder curve of spine. But another part of her couldn't stand that closeness.

She tried to stay still on her back.

She tried to place the rooms within the house, which basement ones fit under which upstairs ones.

She imagined Duke staring at her right up through the ceiling. She shivered, rubbed her arms, tried to calm herself.

But no, that couldn't be right.

Recreating the half-grass view from the two casement windows by his bed downstairs, she realized that that room was just below her own bedroom.

"Doll." "Honey Pie." "Hey Miss."

If only she'd put up her bathing suit. Why had she left her suit down?

She thought about things her mom said sometimes, about boys and girls being different, boys and girls, men and women–the way boys got so mad, the way men got carried away, "carried away."

She began to cry for the first time since Duke had touched her. She tried to keep quiet, but in the midst of her crying, a newspaper her mother had been reading fluttered from the side of the bed to the floor. The unexpected noise raised a scream in her heart. What was that? On the stairs?

Arne's voice. "What a fool, what a fool, what a fool," he said.

Oh. Talking in his sleep. Why did he do that? Her mom said— "teenage boys!" But why did he say 'fool?'

She held her arms about her waist. She felt cold, cold, rubbed her arms. She tried to think of her father. He was round and soft and bald and warm and had warm soft hair on his arms, and a warm soft smell he carried with him, and stared into the air strangely when he was thinking hard, solving a problem. When she was little he used to kneel beside her bed and tell her a story. He only had one story– about a genie and a great blue vase—and after telling it to her he said the Lord's Prayer, the words solemn orbs that hovered above the frog in his throat, lining up into a long drawl of trespasses and bread. She seemed to remember the words not as words, but as sounds, one leading to the next, like the stone slabs of a path, like the second hand on a watch, ticking, ticking, always knowing which way to go.

* * *

Duke was making breakfast. He wore a frilly apron he'd dug up from somewhere. It had been a joke the first days he was there, the strangeness of the net ruffle over his square shoulders. Now the joke was run out but he still wore it, almost seeming to forget its ill fit.

Her mother was late for school and hustled in and out of the kitchen with one of her dad's shirts tossed over her slip to retrieve rubberized curlers from a steaming pot on the stove. Because the curlers made the room so hot, Duke turned the fan on. Its hum was very loud and seemed to add to the energy spattering about the room, grease from a frying pan.

"Ouch," her mother said, "ooh," dropping a curler that was too hot back into the pan.

"Move out of the way huh?" Duke muttered. "Can't you see there's some real cooking going on here?"

Arne chomped his cereal, rubbed his nose and read a newspaper he subscribed to—"Coin World"–rubbed his nose again. Summer was allergy season.

Les only looked up at Duke when she was sure he looked away from her. This was easy. He looked away from her most of the time. Small red patches glowed upon his cheeks as he concentrated upon the scrambled eggs.

He watched the eggs as if they were a book, Les thought, though he never read books, only the newspaper.

The toast popped up, one piece cascading over the side.

"Whoops, here, Arne, you want some toast," Duke said, bouncing the pieces in his palm like a hot potato.

"Excuse me," she said and slid through the narrow space beside her chair.

She went into her room and lay down. It was a new bed, new to her. The mattress used to be Arne's, a double. To make it hers they got a brass headboard and a new puffy bed spread. The whole thing felt too high.

She rolled off it and lay down upon the green sculpted rug, smelling wool and dust.

When she was younger, she used to run from the door of the room to her bed, her real bed. As she got near to the bed, she leapt, landing on the bed in a horizontal roll like a high jumper. The point was to escape any hands lurking under the bed, the man or monster who lived down there when he wasn't in the closet.

She closed her eyes.

Did it hurt her mother? Did she let them do hurting things to her?

Or was it different when you grew up? Like the bad smell of cigarettes, the bitter taste of coffee, hot hot water in a bath–did it all feel different to someone grown?

She couldn't imagine her dad hurting her mother. He was different.

And her mother, she was different too. Not pretty, not trying to please. Hardly like a girl at all, a woman. Talking about politics all the time. Working. With her long hard nose.

She wiped her hands over her face, pulling the skin in two directions like a butterfly's wings, flattening, smoothing. She pressed harder above her eyes first, then under them.

Glenda, a kind of silly girl at school, had told them about a man coming into her room with a knife and she'd screamed and they'd chased him all the way to Marlowe Heights shopping center. If she hadn't screamed, Glenda kept saying. But later Les had heard that the whole story was made up.

She was afraid to look at him, but if he looked at her, it might be all right.

There was still quite a bit to be done on the downstairs. Her mother wanted shelves by the washing machine, something to keep all the boxes off the floor, she said, and after that–

If he didn't look at her all that time–

"Oh" her mom said, pushing open her door, "you're in here." She walked directly over to the closet and began leafing through the back of it where some of her extra clothes were stored.

"Do I have to eat breakfast, Mom?" she asked.

"Mmmm?" her mother said as she pulled out a multiple skirt hanger.

"Which looks best, sweetie?" She stepped around Les to put the hanger down on the bed.

"The beige?" she said holding one skirt in front of her body—

She wished in that instant that her mother didn't work, never worked. She wished her mother were like other mothers. They didn't work. They stayed home and smiled. They cleaned house. They made their kids have chores. Their houses smelled like kale and cleaning fluid and, on special nights, spaghetti sauce. Everything had a place in their house, and everything stayed in its place. You weren't allowed to take something out of its, but if you did, you had to put it back; you just had to.

She didn't want to go to the swimming team, even the pool; thought of walking down to the new houses at the base of her neighborhood to see some of her school friends. Couldn't face school friends. Went over to their next door neighbor's house finally, Carrie and Nancy, old friends that went to the Catholic school.

It was a hot day but they stayed in the basement, where it was cool and dank and checkered with grey and black tiles, eating ice tray popsicles out of grape koolaid. They'd been friends forever, not at school really, not as they were older, but at home, on the street, in their yards, knock knock can Nancy and Carrie come out to play.

They didn't really need to talk much, played cards.

She thought her mother was coming home early but it seemed like no one was there when she got back. She called into the front door and no one answered. She was afraid to go inside, so went around the back way to check out the driveway where Duke always parked to see if his car was there, but as she slipped through the bushes onto the patio, there he was himself, sitting on one of the lawn chairs.

"Uncle Duke." She looked away quickly, trying to stop her face from jerking into something fearful, then looked back at him, trying to seem as if she'd been looking at him all along.

"Yeah, it's Uncle Duke," he said, "what about it?" His face was flat and hard. It wasn't looking anywhere at all.

She didn't know what to say to that, what to do. She didn't want to walk right next to him, but she didn't want to seem to be staying by the bushes either.

She thought suddenly of base, babysitting the base, one two three get off my father's apple tree. So stupid, she thought, how could she be so stupid?

But then he spoke again, his voice lighter. "Hey doll, just the girl I wanted to see. You want to go for a little walk?"

What? She tried to get it straight. One two three, get off–

"You want to go for a walk?" he said again.

What did he mean? What did he want? Duke walked on a golf course, he walked in a bowling alley, he stumped sheetrock around the basement. When he wanted to go somewhere, he drove.

"Hey, come on, let's go for a walk. I want to take you for a walk," he said getting up. He took her wrist firmly.

Her lower body chilled. Stop it stop it let go of me, it said, but she couldn't speak.

Pulling her by the wrist, he moved her across the patio, towards the lawn chair. She didn't say yes or no, she didn't move or not move, only tried to control the surge of cold in her pelvis.

He pulled the back door over the warp in the patio, pushing at the creaking screen. He did all of that easily with one hand while the other spread across both her wrists, trussed her arms together.

She fell down onto her knees, scraping them against the sharp white stucco of the patio.

"God damn it girl. Get up god damn it."

She started to cry. "I have to pee," she said. "Duke, I really really have to pee."

"If you have to pee, god damn it, go and pee."

He pushed his hands into his pockets and walked several steps away. As he moved, the screen door collapsed, banging her side. Though it didn't hurt much, she cried out louder in the midst of the other crying.

"Jesus," he said. "Jesus Mary Mother of God."

She felt something change in him again. He wiped his hands over his head and turned back to her. He reached out for her hand, which she didn't give to him. He took it anyway.

"Aw, come on Les," he whispered. Putting his other hand under her arm, he helped her up. He seemed himself now, rather his hero self, his khaki pants like those of a soldier in a jungle movie.

"Are you okay, doll?" he said. "Gee, look at that. Wow, you really got some bad ones."

Both knees were bleeding. She was crying. Her stomach and thighs were so cold inside. He picked her up easily. He hugged her, pressing her head down to his shoulder and against his bicep. She didn't feel right with her head pressed down there, like a baby and too close. She tried as unobtrusively as possible to pull her head back. But he put his hand against it, the rumple of her hair, and pressed it down again. She felt her panties pressed against his leather belt, his arm below her bottom.

"No," she said, as he carried her into the dark of the basement. "I don't want to."

"Ssshh," he said. "Come on now, don't cry."

"Duke," she said, "I don't want to."

"Look," he said. "I'm not going to touch you. I don't even want to be inside the same goddamn house with you. Look, I'm not going to touch you like that ever again."

She was quiet.

"Look," he said. "We both know what happened the other day, you and I, but it isn't ever going to happen again and we're not going to talk about it either."

He sat her down at the bathroom door. She saw past him to the cellar part of the basement, the gray concrete darkness he had not tried to finish over.

"Now, go inside and pee," he said, "and when you come out we'll fix up your knees."

She looked down at her legs. Blood trailed down her right shin. She looked up to him again.

Big open face. Blue eyes looking down at her, intent but vacant. He nodded toward the bathroom.

"Okay," she said, and gently shut the light wooden door.

She sat down on the toilet, careful of her bleeding knees. She put her feet on the lavender tub, following the edge of white caulk he had redone. She shivered, rubbed her arms.

She thought now that she didn't really have to pee, that she had just felt that way.

She worried that he was listening. She seemed to see his body through the thin wooden door, a silhouette in the marbleized tan of the wood. A great fear rose up in her stomach that he was going to throw open the door, march over and actually force the pee out of her.

She wished she had locked the door, though she knew she never could have. How could she lock a door with him right next to it?

A slow trickle, speeding up to a stream.

Thank you, God.

She got up quickly now, not wanting to make him madder. Washed her hands quickly. She didn't always wash her hands, but she thought he might be listening for it. Hurry, don't make him wait, she thought.

But when she went out, he was not standing anywhere near the door.

"Duke," she called. "Duke?" She was answered by the echo of dust on maple furniture, pine woodwork.

"Duke?"

She felt as if something were about to jump out at her, and could hardly bear to move. She wouldn't go to the back room where his bed was, no, but outside, that would be it. She hurried past the doorway that opened to the cellar part of the basement.

"Duke? Are you here?

"Duke, it's not funny," she called.

The backdoor was ajar. She pulled hard through the place that stuck and was out with a bang. She breathed deeply the humid air. She felt okay outside. She felt okay where there were places to run to.

She rubbed her arms. Although her shirt was soaked with sweat, her arms were covered with goose bumps.

She had practically forgotten about her legs. As she moved forward in the light, she felt almost surprised to see the stains. Some of the blood was dried already, even beginning to flake off. So quickly?

She tiptoed, hopped, over the stucco, because it was rough and hot and hurt her bare feet. But once she began tiptoeing and hopping, she felt light (the blood already dried), so light, and kept it up through the dirt path around the bushes and into the grass of their side yard.

Then she saw that his car was gone, the gravel drive empty, the neighbor's neat hedge on one side, her father's hurly-burly of green-ery on the other.

She ran to the edge of the drive, looking up and down for the tail of his car. But the street was still. Houses blinkered, and the bushes, even grass, hunkered down as if conserving themselves against the heat.

She pushed herself through that weighted stillness–up the hill, up to the front lawn.

He wasn't there either.

She walked down the bit of hill again to her old red swing set that stood at the edge of the yard on that side, sheltering between hedge and tree trunks. There was no swing anymore, the set leprous with rust. She hitched herself up on a side bar.

She should go back in the basement to check on his suitcase, she thought. Though she knew she wouldn't, didn't need to. The suitcase would be gone.

She felt dizzy with the strangeness of it.

She swung her legs back and forth, looking down to the dirt patch below her, looking for something else to think about, something else to feel, something plain and flat and simple.

A part of her was happy that he was gone. Yes, she couldn't help it, she was happy. That she wouldn't have to take a walk with him, talk to him, even see him.

But another part of her could hardly bear it. That he was gone. That he wouldn't come up to her, tease her: "Look at you, dancing about on those sore knees"

That part still wanted him to take her hand, just hand, and like the old days, walk her up the lawn, matching his steps to hers, marveling how she could do so much and look so pretty. That part wanted him to take her inside, upstairs not down, and once inside, lift her up to the kitchen counter, his face smelling of cigars and hair oil, wanted him to wash her knees and bandage them and say, 'see, look how your Uncle Duke can take care of you', perhaps even telling her the story of how her mother had left her with him once when she was a little baby and how he'd diapered and changed her and kept her happy with just a bottle of water all day long and what an immense voice she'd had back then, what lungs—my land he thought she'd be some kind of opera singer—

That part of her wanted to be just that little again, and for him to be that big.

Arne
Suburban Maryland
July 1968

A rne hammered the stake so hard he kept missing it, the hammer thudding dully into the grass.

"You know, Arne, well, it might work better not to hit it so hard," his father said.

Arne kept his gaze turned from his father. He could picture how he was standing right now and hated it–his legs pressed close together so that his pants rumpled, his weight shifting from one foot to the other, his hands pushed deep into his back pockets.

This was his dad's way of saying that he felt bad because he would not let Arne do what Arne wanted. That he had had to say no embarrassed him, brought out his most awkward, bashful self.

"It's just idiotic to camp in a back yard when there are woods just a couple of blocks away," Arne grumbled.

"I just want to make sure you can operate the tent, that's all," his father said. "It's not so easy, this old army kind. It's strong, sure, you get caught in the rain you won't even feel a drop; that is if it's not a real dousing, but it's not easy to put up, that's for sure."

"It's not the rain I'm worrying about," Arne said, "it's suffocation."

"Oh Daddy, if it rains, those two will come creeping into the house anyway, I know them."

"Come on, Les, just because you can't come."

She stuck out her tongue at him.

"Well, you can't."

As Arne pulled the rope over the stake, the tent stumbled to a crouch. He could feel his dad aching to bend down beside him, to, in his slow and seemingly fumbling way, get it all done right. But he'd already made that much clear at least, no help with the tent–he didn't even want his dad next to him right now.

"It's not real woods up there anyway," his dad said. "Oh, it looks like woods, sure." He pulled his slightly rounded nose. "But, well, you know–"

The woods were a barrier, a no man's land, between their rows of suburban houses and Saint Barnabas Road, a street of poor houses, broken-down shacks, where the colored people lived.

There hadn't been rioting there. But even Arne knew that things felt different these days, a kind of anger that you felt could come spurting out, now matter what you believed in.

Still. "At least we could have a fire," he said, tugging at the tent ropes.

His father's mouth pulled down. "You know how Mom is," he said. "She doesn't want to get the lawn ruined for just one night. And she's in a bad mood anyway, because of Duke, you know, the basement."

"If she won't let us go anywhere she should at least let us have a fire."

"Arne, look at all these houses. I don't even know if it's legal to have a fire like that–uncontained. We don't want the fire department breathing down our necks."

Arne shrugged, knotting the rope around the stake. Who cared about a fire? Once the thing was in your back yard.

"You know I'd be happy to drive you guys, while the Lowells get their car fixed," his father said. "If the Lowells still want to go to Shadyside."

"Da-ad–"

"I know it's too late tonight," his father went on, hands protesting. "But, I don't know, tomorrow maybe. Those little Lowell girls can't take up that much room, that Dodge Dart is bigger than you think."

Arne tried to get the knot right, to pull hard enough to get the slump out of the tent's middle. "It's not the girls, it's their grandmother."

"Oh yeah. I forgot about the grandmother."

Arne sat back to his knees. It was late but the humid grip of the day hadn't loosened. He felt a sweat bead over his forehead like a slick on a puddle. Shit. He took the bottom of his T-shirt and pressed it to his face.

Goddamn Jasper anyway. Just because it was in his yard didn't mean he should have to do the whole stupid thing.

"You want me to hold something?" Les asked. She had been sitting on her knees quietly, pulling up grass around the pup tent and making a little pile.

They should have just stayed at the pool, Arne thought, eaten their stupid plastic cheeseburgers and then, if they were going to sleep in the yard, just dragged some sleeping bags out at the last minute. It was too hot for the tent anyway, which was his stupid father's idea to begin with. 'I know!' he'd said when stupid Shadyside had fallen through–

"I can pull this rope, look," Les said, taking hold of something that seemed to straighten up the back of the dark green hulk.

"Leave it alone."

"Please."

"Drop it."

"Here, Les," his dad said. "Why don't you help me get the charcoals started?"

"Hey Buddy." It was Jasper.

Just seeing his friend made Arne feel lighter. He was such a smiler. His eyes crinkled into curves and he had this big tan mole that practically covered the base of his cheek, just next to his dimple.

It was funny, that mole; it might have looked ugly on someone else, but on Jasper it was a mark of distinction, one more sign of good will. It made him, as Leslie once said, look like a human teddy bear.

"Hey Les," Jasper called out.

"Jasper!" Leslie coming out from the patio where she and her dad were working on the outdoor grill.

God damn her, Arne thought, hating the she always flounced around, always wanting to be in the center of everything. Okay, she was being quiet enough right now, but why couldn't she just go away? He bent over the tent with exaggerated concentration.

"So, Arne, we're really going to do this, huh?" Jasper smiled.

"I guess so," Arne said. "Seems kind of dumb in a back yard."

"No, it'll be great," Jasper said. He squatted down next to Arne–

"So what it's a back yard. We can spook around the neighborhood, you know what I mean," he whispered. "John's going out with that girl Cheryl tonight. Try to catch up with them."

Arne groaned inside. Jasper was just too goofy sometimes.

"Honest, I think he's going to hose her," Jasper said.

What? Jesus.

"God, Jasper, how about just shutting up, huh?"

Jasper looked around, genuinely uncertain of the reason for Arne's irritation.

Arne punched him lightly in the shoulder, his gaze pointing towards Leslie. "Duhhh!"

"What, her?" Jasper said. "She knows the score, doesn't she?"

"Let's just be quiet till they all clear out," Arne said. "Go on, Les, get out of here."

Leslie scrunched her shoulders around her neck and put her arms around her waist. She got up and walked over by the apple tree, looking up at the early fruit. She left so easily because she was just pretending not to hear them, Arne thought.

The dark green tent surrendered itself at last to a dismal and seemingly permanent slump. Arne pulled on the ropes again, hard, but it didn't seem to make any difference.

"Shit," he said. "Do we need this?"

"Naw, it's too hot anyway."

"It's buggy enough."

"Yeah, but we have to breathe."

"Yeah."

His father stepped around from behind the big forsythia bush at the edge of the patio.

"Well, hello Jasper. Hey, look here, I got these charcoals going, boys. Now, all you have to do is let it sit for a while."

"Hi Mr. Undset," Jasper said. "How are you tonight? Gee, thanks a lot for letting us stay here."

Arne felt his skin crawl at Jasper's politeness. Yes, he was wrong, he was wrong to be the way he was, mean, rude, disrespectful. Yes, yes, he knew it; yes, okay, he was wrong.

"Oh, ah, well, that's okay, Jasper," his father said, smiling with pleasure and embarrassment. "No trouble. No trouble at-tall. I'm just sorry I couldn't take you guys out to your place, uh–you know, by the Chesapeake. You know I'd be happy to drive, even lend your dad my car if it'd do any good."

"Nah, that's okay, Mr. Undset. My dad's getting his fixed this week. No big deal."

"Yes, well, if there's anything I can do," Arne's father said, rubbing the top of his bald head. "You sure you don't want me to help you with this, Arne." Then laughed towards Jasper. "I guess you boys are old enough to want to do things like this for yourself."

"It's okay, Dad," Arne said. "We're fine."

"Maybe you should leave on the patio light, you know, when it gets dark? You want the patio light on?"

"We'll take care of it, Dad."

"Okay, well..." stepping towards the door, "oh yeah–make sure the charcoals are put out, okay? Really out. Not smoking or anything."

"We'll make sure, Dad."

"You know, you really might want that light. You don't want to trip over a tent stake or something. I know it sounds silly, but in the dark–"

"Dad–"

"Okay," his father chuckled. "I guess I should just let you boys be now."

"Yeah, how about it?" Arne said.

"Have a good time."

"Goodbye Les," Arne sang to his sister (now slinking around the grill.)

"Arne–"

"Out."

"Please."

"Now," he said, holding the door open.

After Les and his Dad left, Arne felt anger flaking off like sunburned skin. The air itself seemed to grow lighter, grayer, and the sounds of the neighborhood, distant crack of bat and growl of lawnmower, to become clearer and softer at once, sounds he could tolerate.

He inhaled deeply. The charcoal smoke reached into his stomach, dangling its promise of cooked meat.

Actually, it was something for his parents to let them cook. Though his father would probably be back to snoop about the fire soon enough.

"Boy, your father sure worries a lot, doesn't he?" Jasper said.

"That's what my father does in life."

"Come on."

"It's true. He thinks up these great physical theories, then shoots them down again with all the things that could go wrong. He also hides out from my mom."

They both stared into the charcoal briquets, little ash pillows piled over a bright orange bed.

Arne put his head in his hands, sniffing the ashen sweat of his palms. "So, you bring any beer?"

"Something better."

Arne felt his heart drop. "What, Wild Turkey?" He didn't really like the hard stuff.

"Dum de dum de dum de dum"

"Come on."

"Well, Arne, my boy, my brother Johnny, he says, how you boys like some grass tonight since you fixing to be laying on it?"

Grass.

Arne didn't trust his voice to answer.

"'How about a little J, man?' he says to me. 'J for Jasper' and he rolls me one himself." Jasper pushed his hand deep into his pocket and pulled out what looked to Arne like a little paper slug. A wrinkled curled-up slug at this point, prone on the flat of his palm.

"See," Jasper said.

To actually see the joint filled Arne with fear. He imagined a police car pulling up to the house, the cops standing Jasper up against the brick wall, then him.

"Hey man," Arne said, "you better put it away."

"No shit," Jasper said, rolling the thing back into his pocket.

"Look, we better get going," Arne said, turning back to the fire. He worked quietly, carefully, over the coals, all the time thinking really fast.

"Les. Le-es," he heard his father call. Made him jump. Christ, what was she up to now?

"Les–"

He looked off to one side of the yard. "Les, if you're around here, you better get yourself gone," he said.

The burgers were sizzling. He flipped them awkwardly, brain jittering.

He'd only smoked pot once before, just a tiny bit, with Jasper and his brother John at a big birthday party the Lowells had had for their grand-mother. They'd gone out back behind the doghouse, Johnny holding and patting the dog half the time to keep it quiet.

He had been really scared; trembling, he remembered, and that the smoking burned his throat. He'd had to clamp down hard on his mouth and lungs to keep from coughing and making a damn fool out of himself.

He hoped it wasn't his asthma did that. He hoped it was just a matter of getting used to it.

Afterwards, well, the feeling was okay, just a kind of softness, silliness. Though he also had had a couple of beers, so it was hard to tell what caused what.

They ate the burgers quickly. Jasper, who was a lot more experienced in these things because of his older brother, kept telling Arne how good grass made things taste, and that they should smoke before they ate, but Arne kept saying no.

"We could probably get away with it with my dad," Arne said, "but my mom has the nose of a hawk"

"We could say we were just burning incense," Jasper said. "Or I've got it. Something to keep away bugs"

"She does read the newspaper, you know."

Jasper hit the bottom of the ketchup bottle. "So what are we going to do?"

"We'll take a walk, that's what."

"Great idea," Jasper said. "Even if we just go behind Miller's tool shed."

"Not behind Miller's," Arne said. "He's the kind to call the cops in a second."

"Oh yeah." Jasper ate avidly, his mole moving in sync with his chews. "But there's got to be someplace."

They finished up quickly, put out the fire, gathered up their plates, their cutlery, models of efficiency and good order. They dragged the hose briskly from the side of the house to the charcoal fire, doing every single thing Arne's dad had said to extinguish it, anxious to finish quickly.

He had always thought of smoking grass as something hippies did, rock stars, the Beatles. He had nothing against hippies, he liked the Beatles, he had just not thought of it as something he would do, math nerd.

Of course, there was John. John had even been in ROTC; wore the little orange ascot, the whole bit. Now, he'd even gotten an ROTC scholarship to college. It was all part of the plan, Jasper said. John could be on ROTC, go to college practically free, and not actually have to serve in the army till he was done. And by that time, four more years, the war was sure to be over

Shit. Arne's stomach turned nervously and he brushed his hands together, wiping away the charcoal dust.

"We better tell them we're going," he said. "Otherwise they'll come look."

"You think they would?"

"My dad?"

Arne went in the back door slowly. You were supposed to be okay as long as you were in school, but what if you got kicked out of school? That was always his mom's big threat, among other things—prison terms, chromosome damage. "Look, at that poor guy that got caught, arrested, thrown out of school and then had to be drafted, even when they let him off."

His folks watched the TV. Folks meaning Les. His mother was not actually watching but scooping water out of the bottom of the second-hand air-conditioner a friend had recently given them. His father was stretched out in his pajamas on the rug, looked asleep.

The room was too yellow after the outdoors, the creamy lamp-shades jaundicing the light. Arne felt huge bursting in, too tall for that ceiling, and conscious, in the moist shiver of air conditioning, of his heavy outdoor scent, the onion smell of his sweat, the rope and ash smell of his hands, a trace of ketchup.

He tried to make himself smaller, stooping his shoulders, bending his head. "I just wanted to let you know we're going to take a little walk before we go to sleep," he said.

"What?" his father's voice started up, alarmed, shaking off the sleep.

"Jasper and I are going to take a walk, just a short one."

"Damn this thing. Why didn't she tell me it was as bad as all that?" his mother said from the window unit. "It'd drip over everything if I didn't scoop it"

"They want to take a walk," Arne's father said to his mom, as if she'd just come in the room. Then, rubbing his eyes, adjusting his glasses, he stumbled to his feet to look out the window.

"You're sure you want to go now?" he turned back to Arne. "It's awful dark out."

"It's not so dark," Arne said. "It just looks it from in here."

"I don't know," his dad said looking at his watch. "The days are get-ting shorter now you know. What do you think, Mama?"

She stopped her scooping a moment, first peering deep into a metal tray that formed the bottom of the air conditioner. Then she too looked over to the uncovered window.

"It's no big deal. Jasper forgot something at his house," Arne said. "We just wanted to run up there a second."

"Oh well, if you're just going up to his house" she said. She picked up the bowl of water, which sat on their wooden stereo below the air conditioner, and wiped under it with a dish towel. "God," she muttered, "just look at this–"

His father's mouth turned a full half circle. "You want me to drive you?"

"*Dad!*"

"Okay, okay. But be careful of cars, huh? They can't see you when it's this dark. You don't have anything white, do you? You should at least wear something light colored"

"Daddy," Leslie joined in, imitating her mother's habitual tone. "They're pretty big."

"Big don't mean a thing when it's pitch black," her father said.

"Can I come?" Leslie asked, addressing herself to Arne. "Please Arne, can I?"

Arne didn't look at her. His father glanced down with a pained expression, then focused on Arne again. "Make sure you walk towards the traffic," he said, his hands chopping the air into lanes. "You know what I mean, on the side of the opposite direction."

His mom rubbed the towel along the stereo, then folded it and put the bowl back on top.

"Don't you think she should stay with us, Ing?" his dad said.

"Who, Les? Oh yes, stay home with us, sweetie," she said, still inspecting the lid of stereo. "You don't want to go out with those boys."

Arne bounded out of there fast. He grabbed the two wooden railings of the basement stairs so he could do ten steps at a shot, practically the whole staircase. He ran out to Jasper who leaned against the brick wall next to the door. Jasper looked so old in the darkness that it stopped him for a moment, the mole like some kind of beard.

"All set?" Jasper asked.

"You got the stuff?"

"Duh! What you should ask is if I've got matches."

"Oh yeah," Arne said, smiling and starting to walk away. "You got matches?"

"Shit." Jasper jumped towards Arne to try to land a punch into his back, then together they ran laughing through the side yard, tore through the end of the hedge, and down the big paved hill that bordered the house, only braking at the corner, resting a minute against a stop sign that looked dark green in that light.

* * *

They acted more sober on the way back, the thrill of anticipation replaced by the slightly drunken absorption of the dope, all tempered by the fear of discovery. It made them walk, at least some of the time, straight as the curb, faces stretched long as the street.

"Hey," Jasper said. "Don't go up this time, you don't want your mom to see your eyes, man."

Arne laughed. "She wouldn't pay attention. Not unless there was a zit sitting right in the middle of them."

"Right smack in the middle," Jasper said dissolving into laughter. "And then she'd squeeze it right?"

"What?"

Jasper laughed and laughed. "I said, 'and then she'd squeeze it right?'"

"Shut up," Arne said.

The street was truly dark now, illuminated only by small geometries of light, which fell like shadow, from the lamps inside houses. That and the occasional television, which shot out a collapsed blue pyramid..

No street lights in their neighborhood, too late in the season for fireflies.

The quiet felt like a glove over the soft feelings inside him. Arne tried consciously to relax into that glove, to stretch out into all its different extensions. Another part of his mind simply refused.

How many people lived in their neighborhood now anyway? How many houses? A lot in the last few years–three hundred? Three-fifty? And in the houses, you figure at least three, really four–he tried to focus on the numbers–three times three hundred, four times three-fifty. As he tried to figure it out, the quiet jumbled, Jasper's sneakers squeaking in out in out like some goddamn tree frog, and with Jasper, this picture of his mother entered, his mother peering into his face to examine what new eruptions marred it. Change that channel. Shit I hate you Jasper, shit you shouldn't talk about squeezing zits, mole face. That huge one all over your back, can't even take your T-shirt off at the swimming pool

"So, hey, Arne, I mean... so, what's it like for you?" Jasper asked.

Arne looked over to Jasper, whose eyes smiled back at him, and now, strangely, powerfully, felt overwhelmed with love. Like he just wanted to hug him. Shit, how'd he take that? he laughed to himself. Call him a faggot.

He laughed. "How quiet it is, I guess, and whether my goddamn folks have crashed yet. What about you?"

"I'm thinking about John and that babe," Jasper snickered, "that Cheryl."

Several lights were on in the house. Arne didn't go upstairs but felt his and Jasper's presence duly noted by his dad from the large picture window upstairs. Then the lights were slowly and sequentially turned off.

He and Jasper lit a citronella candle and sat on their sleeping bags beside the pup tent. The candle, sunk inside a green bulb-shaped glass, covered with plastic fishnet, reminded Arne of the candles at the cocktail lounge at the officers' club. He hadn't actually been to the cocktail lounge; they only went to the Club for an occasional Sunday dinner, but he'd seen it. "The Cove" in brownish cursive letters, a big dark room with burlap bags, nets, shells and driftwood pinned upon the walls.

That bar always seemed so lonely, so dark, the silhouette of wait-ress, apron, drinks, the customers up against some wall. He lay down on his bag and looked up at the sky.

The sky was dark too, but bluish. What they called midnight blue, he supposed. He looked up above the frame of his glasses and then through his glasses, measuring the radii of the blurred starlight. His throat still burned from the grass but the rest of his body felt like velvet, as if the thick quiet air had hunkered down into a form that was himself. As if he had become a quark, he smiled, one of those black holes.

He used to be interested in astronomy and knew the constella-tions. He did not trace them now, but simply concentrated on how the softness of the starlight compared to the softness in his skin, looking alternately over his glasses and through them until he realized that this was a habitual gesture of his father's, comparing his natural and corrected vision. He stopped immediately, turned over onto his stomach, and pressed the side of his face against the worn cowboys who stormed across the sleeping bag's inner flannel.

He noticed from this angle that the upstairs bathroom light was still on, a fluorescent brilliance reflecting grey tiled walls, enamel paint. Probably his dad's idea of a nightlight, he thought. Then, his mother's face and shoulders, red from the bath, filled the window frame.

He pulled his head up sharply, surprised you could see so much. Boy, look at that. God, Mom. Jesus, pull down the stupid blinds.

He looked over quickly to make sure Jasper wasn't seeing her too.

His mother shook her hair, which looked wet and curly, from one side of her head to the other. Cleaning her ears? But could you see her breasts? That's all he really cared about. He stretched his neck out, though he didn't really want to see his mother's breasts. He had a sense of his mother's breasts, fairly large, fairly droopy, reddish–but he did want to see if you could see them.

But no, you couldn't really, and now, she... was gone, no, just the top of her head–now gone. A minute later the window went dark.

"Arne, hey Arne," Jasper said urgently, "you still awake?"

"Shit yes." He looked sharply into Jasper's face for some reflection of his mom's breasts.

"Great," Jas giggled, "I thought you'd bopped off there for a while." He pulled, seemingly from the depths of his sleeping bag, a khaki-covered canteen. "You want some water?"

"Okay."

Arne wasn't really thirsty, but the sight of the canteen did bring a certain craving. He loved canteens, that warm pipe-tinged water. He took a long sip, wiped his lips on his arm, handed it back.

A car drove by the side street, its lights roaming a swathe of sky like a searchlight. Arne could feel Jasper watching it with him, and in the moment after, that they shared the renewed darkness.

"So Arne, "Jasper said. "You think John is screwing that babe, what do you want to bet?" He held his arm up close to his eyes squinting over his watch. "I'd say right about now." He swung his other arm down to his side as if he were starting a race, then began to laugh wildly.

"Jesus, Jasper, I don't know. Does she like him?"

"You've seen her, haven't you? At the pool. Oh Johnny!'" he made his voice high and lilting. "The way she's always running after him up in the chair. Then her swimming like that, you know, during the rest period."

"Swimming like what?"

"Oh you know. She does all these underwater acrobat things."

"She does?"

"Haven't you seen her? Oh yeah, then diving off the high dive. Christ the other day her top comes off and everything; whew, she was so embarrassed, her big boobs. It's like she might have just gone up to him, said 'here, you want to try one.'" Jasper giggled, folding into himself.

Arne simultaneously felt his dick hardening and his ears turning a deep hot red. Shit. He hated Jasper. He didn't want to hear all this stuff from him.

That wasn't exactly true. He did want to hear it. But right now–

It was just so weird with the grass, like he was both feeling it inside himself and imagining himself to feel it, standing beside himself watching his dick grow into a huge club, huge, like the throbbing swollen thumb in a cartoon.

"Yeah, like 'here Johnny, just take a feel.'" Jasper said again, laughing.

What he wished was that Jasper would say all this stuff in one room and he could sit listening in another room. With his hand on his dick, sure if he wanted it, just not right next to the guy.

He thought about the girl Jasper spoke of, that Cheryl. She did have good breasts. They curled around the triangles of her bikini like a grownup woman's. Almost, well not really, but a little bit like those women in the magazines. Though her stomach was just as round, that was the trouble with her. She looked really dumpy walking around the pool, a big duck, and this thick nose; there was something about her nose

"So Arne," Jasper said quietly, "you gotta tell me now, well, you know?"

"What?" Arne felt his cock deflate immediately.

"You know."

"You gotta give me a hint, Jas."

"I mean I know you haven't screwed around!" Jasper turned his head back again sharply. "I mean I don't think so. You would have told me that, right?"

"Jasper," Arne pulled a stern face, thinking, God, Jasper. But he couldn't hold it. "Jasper," he said laughing.

"Okay, so you haven't done that right?"

"Duh."

"So what have you done?"

"Jasper, you idiot," Arne really laughed now. He made a big point of laughing, rolling over onto the sleeping bag.

"Come on," Jasper said. "It's not so funny as that"

"I'm sorry. It's just well, look, Jas. I've been living on the same street as you all these years right?"

"Right."

"Going to the same schools?"

"Right."

"And screwing the same girls," Arne laughed.

Jasper groaned, then he too collapsed in laughter.

What? Arne jumped up

"Shit Les, goddamn it, get the hell out of there." he said.

She was kneeling behind the tent.

He wiped his face. "Jesus, Les. Goddamn that scared me. Shit. How long have you been sitting there?"

"Hey Les," Jasper smiled.

"Arne, I'm sorry," she burst out. "I didn't mean to scare you. I just wanted to bring you down some of those rice krispie things. I got Mom to let me make you some for dessert."

She had a small plate of rice krispie marshmallow squares stacked up in front of her.

"Hey Les, great," Jasper said, leaning over the plate. "Perfect timing."

"Jasper!"

"Oh come on, Arne, she just wants to be part of things for a little bit. Right Les?"

She nodded.

"You don't know what it's like to be the younger kid," Jasper went on, using his fingers as calipers to take hold of three rice krispies squares at once.

"I just don't want her," Arne said.

"Please Arne," Les' voice bordered on the tearful. "Just a little while. Just to see the candle."

He turned away.

"Mom and Dad have already gone to bed, they won't know..." She paused. "I brought you a beer," she said, reaching from behind her legs to bring out a Budweiser.

"That's it, she's in," Jasper crowed.

Arne took the can. "Where'd you get that?"

"It was the one left over, you know."

"Oh yeah, from Duke."

They held their collective breath as Arne pulled off the top. It sounded so loud in that stillness that they looked instantly up to the house's windows, sleepless but blank.

Arne took the first sip, a long one. It was really cold, good. He didn't much like the taste warm. He handed it to Jasper, then sat back down on his sleeping bag.

"Can I sit on your bag with you, Arne?" Les asked.

"Sure, well, I want to lie down," he said. "But there's still room on the side.".

As Arne sipped the cold beer, he felt happier. She was a good girl, Les. He liked the feel of her leaning against his legs, he liked the look of her sitting there so long-haired and so small-faced, the candlelight on her nose, cheeks and forehead. Now *she* was a really pretty girl, he thought, not like that Cheryl. He felt glad suddenly to have a sister like her.

Les passed the beer back and forth between the boys, not drinking any herself. No need to do too much passing after a while, Jasper concentrating on the marshmallow treats.

"So Les," Jasper asked, as he chomped krispies. "How's life treating you these days?"

She pulled up a couple of handfuls of grass. "Okay, I guess."

"You like that Mr. Lazlo? He's a real ballbuster, I heard. Oops," Jasper chuckled, wiped his mouth on his arm, "I mean, slavedriver."

"He's okay," she said. "I like it when we swim with all our clothes on."

"Oh yeah?"

"And then when you take them off, you feel so fast."

Arne sighed. "You want to go to sleep soon?" he said to Jasper.

"Just a minute. These are so good." He grabbed one more square of rice krispies.

The air filled with Jasper's chews. Arne lay straight back, shut his eyes. Though there was something else in the air too, something smelled so sweet. The rice krispie treats?

No, it was apples, on the tree, on the ground too probably. Early for them, but then they were always early. Banana apples, his mother called them, because they were softish, he supposed and yellow and got ripe so early, in summer instead of the fall, got ripe when it was still hot out. Stupid name.

"You better go up now, Les."

* * *

His mother started dinner early the next day. She had reached a break in her paper and wanted to make something special. Sukiyaki. This was kind of a new thing, a cardboard package holding a can of chinesey stuff that she added a lot of fresh stuff to, though you didn't have to.

A new product, new in the stores, though his parents liked it so much because it reminded them of something old, something they had had before. This was their favorite quality in anything–that it reminded them of something else, something nostalgic. For his father especially. He thought anything the second time around was good, even if the first time was hell.

"Say Mama," his dad said beaming next to the open can of chinese vegetables. "That smells just like that place, remember it? In Hopkins, the Moon Palace." Arne groaned.

His mother chopped celery with a grim concentration. His mother did not particularly like to cook. His mother did not particularly like anything as far as he could tell except to read the newspaper and to buy new clothes. Oh she liked her family all right, he supposed; she loved Leslie, but in terms of things to do

Since he'd grown older, Arne liked to try and imagine his parents having sex. "Andrew, not like that," he imagined his mother saying, just like she did whenever his father did anything.

Though sometimes he imagined her to be very shy–in that one area–unable to even complain. His dad too.

In fact, that seemed most likely of all–that they were like two blind people pretending they didn't know either each other or what was going on. "Oh excuse me" after his dad inserted his cock.

"God Andrew," his mother said, "could you please get out of the kitchen, you just take up so much room somehow, I can hardly breathe."

Arne looked up from the table at his mother's back and shoulders squared over her chopping block. She'd gone to the pool today and still wore her bathing suit. She'd gotten so much sun that a field of freckles stood out against the swell of reddened shoulders, back. He looked away from her legs, the upper part crinkled like a mass of crepe paper.

"Gee Dad, I'm sorry, but please," she said, "you just have this way of crowding me."

"God dang it, Ing, I'm only trying to help. You say you never get any help all the time. Don't you want me to set the god danged table."

"Do I want to hear you clanging the dishes around? No. Breaking them? No. Using kooky silverware? No. And careful of my feet."

His father stepped back so sharply it looked as if he were about to totter over. But his voice grew stronger, dropped the midwestern twang. "God damn it, Ing, there's just no helping you. There's not a damn way in the world some one can help."

Shut up, Arne screamed inside, but only gripped the sides of the newspaper tightly, bending further into it, trying to concentrate on grain futures. The stock market and the commodities markets were his new fascination, that, and speculating in coins. It was all money. How to make as much as possible as quickly as possible. Everything was going up fast what with the war.

His mother poured the row of celery chunks into the frying pan, wiping her bangs from her eyes as she tended it. His father did not leave the kitchen, but tried to do exactly what he'd been doing before, only more quietly. Except his quietness, a grinding of black shoes against linoleum, shuffling pants' legs, clicking porcelain, seemed to simply concentrate all the intensity of his previous noise so as to make each movement even more annoyingly audible.

Arne tried harder to focus on the news. Grains futures.

His father tapped him on the shoulder, gesturing with his head towards a pitcher of lemonade he carried.

"Okay," Arne sighed grudgingly.

Sshh, his father smiled eying Ingrid, then he poured the glass he carried in his other hand so full, it dripped down the side. "Oops," he mouthed, looking quickly at Ingrid.

Arne looked too.

But she was distracted. No, more than that, his father was back inside the circle again, the magic circle of mother approval.

"Andrew," she said, crinkling her nose at the frying pan. "Do you think it would be good with bell pepper?"

Not able to stand anymore, Arne, lemonade in hand, went back outside to the tent. Had to take it down anyway.

Les was sitting out on the grass there already, squinting into the worn folds of some thick paperbook. *Gone With the Wind* probably. So stupid.

"Hey Les, you can help, you know."

"Sure."

They worked quietly. The stakes were a bitch, the wood rubbing the inside of his hand raw. Les' must be a lot worse, he thought, but when he looked over to her, she seemed to be paying little attention to her hands, her cheeks red with pulling.

It made him feel good that he could pull the stakes up and she couldn't–even if she was a girl–and he picked up the pace of his work.

"Here, you start winding up the rope," he said, taking over her stake. "Oh great." It threw him back as it came out, like some long wooden onion. "What a waste."

He crawled into the tent and came out with the beer can.

"I'll take care of this," he said.

"Wait a second."

"What?"

"Can you talk to me a second?" She sat down just by the sagging entrance to the tent. He looked down at her. Now that he had stopped moving, he could smell the strong scent of his sweat. The smell made him uncomfortable, anxious to just get done and inside again.

"Can't it wait till we finish this shit?"

"I kind of wanted to ask you right away," she said, pulling at tufts of grass in front of the tent.

"Well, okay, I guess," he said. He sat down sluggishly, shading his eyes with his hands.

God, he was tired. Even with the grass and the beer, he hadn't really slept. He leaned over to retrieve the glass of lemonade, took a sip. Christ, even just sitting next to that stupid tent raised your temperature ten degrees.

"Arne," she said. "Is it true what you said to Jasper about you and he, you know, doing that?"

"Doing what?"" He instilled his voice with a tone of cool irritation even as his mind swerved.

"You know," she said, flushed face still focusing on the stupid lawn. "I mean you guys haven't really been, you haven't been really doing anything–with girls?"

Oh Jesus. What an idiot.

He stood up, brushing the grass she'd pulled up off his knees and thighs. "I gotta throw out this can."

But she caught him. She put her hands on his old chucks, her head down by the rumpled shoestrings.

"Arne," she said. "Tell me."

"Come on, Les, don't be goofball."

She didn't move.

"Come on Les," he said bending down and pulling her arms to get her hands off of his feet. "I just want to get this stupid tent down and go inside to the air conditioning. Can't you just come on?" In all this, his hands on her arms, he couldn't help noticing how cool her flesh was, and soft. He realized he had hardly ever touched her. How could she be so cool with him so sweaty?

"Arne," she went on, keeping her face by his feet. "Is it bad if something happens to you? I mean, if you sort of let it happen?"

"What do you mean?"

"Like if you're a girl and you let someone–"

Those girls. Shit. Feeling each other up or what? He felt his cock twitch, and wanted to curse himself, them too.

He'd come in on them once lying on the bed downstairs. It was mainly that Carrie, he thought, too old for Les and too dumb.

"God Les, why do you girls do that stuff? Shit, you know better than that."

She tore the grass in little tiny clumps. He could see tears dropping onto them. God, she was just a kid. He sat down opposite her. So stupid.

"I don't think Duke is coming back," she said. "He'll probably never come back."

Duke? God damn it, what was she talking about—

"Jesus, Les," he said. "You shouldn't play with those girls if they do some weird shit. That stupid Carrie."

"It wasn't–it wasn't Carrie."

His mind filled, unaccountably, with Johnny Lowell, Jasper's brother, imagining his zinc-nosed figure in the lifeguard's chair, slapping one thick freckled knee

"That's why he left," she whispered.

"What the hell? Duke? Did he try to borrow money from you? You can't lend him money, Les. You know what mom says. Christ, did he really try to get some?"

Her face still turned away. He looked at the top of her head, the blonde hair parting in the middle at the front, then crawling to the side as it extended. He tried to see money in that part, Duke's borrowing money.

Instead, he pictured Duke hitting her. Slapping her so hard that she fell down, himself rushing in to take a hold of Duke's arms as he'd seen boys do when others were fighting, 'come on Duke, calm down god damn it'

He felt as if an iron vest had been clamped over his chest.

"Did you tell Mom?"

She shook her head no.

"Do you want me to say something? I don't know, tell her you need to talk?"

"No," she said. "It would make her too upset."

He sighed. He knew what she meant. They would never hear the end of it.

They put everything away in a basement closet. Not one of the ones that Duke built. An old one, built into the pine wall, hardly visible.

It was musty inside, a distillation of basement. At the top hung his father's old World War II uniforms, winter darks, summer lights, small, too small for his father now. They looked both stiff and limp on the hangers, starched in the distant past.

Below them were clumps of unidentifiable stuff. He jammed the tent into the midst of it, pushing hard on the folds as if the tent were something he pressed into an overfull garbage can.

Normally, when he went into that closet he felt a thrill of pride at the sight of the uniforms. That for all his Dad's awkwardness, his shyness, his scientist's hesitation, he had worn these uniforms for several years, marched his body around two hemispheres, worn a pack, carried a gun, shaved out of a cup, probably killed people too, though he couldn't really imagine that; but he must have raised a gun to his shoulder, right? He just had to. Before he got transferred into the rocket unit.

Now the smell of the closet made him sick. He rubbed his nose. Even his eyes seemed to be tearing.

Les looked deeply inside it. He stepped in front of her, blocking her view, pressing the closet door shut hard, jamming the long bolt through the metal loop on the other side.

Stupid stupid girl.

A sob caught in his throat, hurt like a fist to swallow. He thought of the back room. When Duke stayed there, he kept everything just so—his clothes hung up, his old green plaid suitcase folded up, a deck of cards on his bedside table.

He wanted to hit her. Not trusting himself, he hurried back through the front of the basement. Stupid stupid girl.

He kept thinking of the way she sat around all day singing, singing Julie Andrews idiot, when you just couldn't take it anymore.

Had he been in the house?

What was it? What the fuck?

"Look, I made a nice dinner for you," his mother said to him. "It won't be any good warmed up."

She turned to his father. "Don't *you* eat so much, Andrew. I didn't mean that you had to make up for Arne."

Just shut up.

"I haven't eaten so much," his father moaned. "Look here." He pointed to a soppy mound of rice and bean threads on his plate. "I've hardly touched a bit of it."

Arne got up and turned on the TV.

"Can't we have a family dinner for once" his mother said, the crease in her forehead deepening, "without the TV?" But Arne paid no attention to her. It was the news. He knew she'd get interested soon enough.

On the screen were pictures of the war, the fluttering of helicop-
ters mainly and, in the blur of moving camera, combat boots, grass,
muddy water, rice paddies probably, thatched houses.

Then the young boy came on. He'd been hit by something; it was
hard to hear what.. The top left hand side of his face was hidden by
incomprehensible dark goo; an explosion covered his eye.

Arne felt his breath, all the breath in the room, stop.

The boy stared into the camera which was a bee, buzzing, hovering, tracing and retracing the wound; it seemed to proffer an irresistible nectar.

His mother cursed.

"Oh God, why do they have to show this now?" his father said.

The picture panned to a far shot through the door of the hut, the
outline of the boy's fine limbs, and then it moved off to another blur of
tall grass, mud, camouflage pants. A GI was being carried in a stretcher,
shoved onto the helicopter over a lot of fast talk, "Charlie", blared shouts.

Then, as every night, came the blue screen with the days' numbers. The announcer spoke beneath a soberly wrinkled forehead.
Arne looked at his sister who watched unblinkingly, though she didn't
normally like the news much.

He saw them in the back room now, Duke holding her in place,
Duke laying her down on the bed, holding her down there.

He felt his dick getting hard, shifted in his seat, crossed his legs.

It didn't make sense, Duke holding her down. Les was always the
good one, the lucky one. She didn't have asthma, bad teachers. It was
like she wasn't even his sister.

He scrunched his legs together. He pulled his feet next to him, his
knees up over his groin.

There was a dog show. Someone had dressed up a dog in pants
that came down over its paws, big flowered bell bottoms and on top,
a short half blouse. It was an Afghan dog, with long hair combed over
its ears and weird sunglasses put on its muzzle. It looked sort of like
Janis Joplin.

His father laughed and laughed. "Look at that. Ingrid, look at
that."

Arne looked at Les who watched the dog with the same intent con-centration she'd just applied to the Vietnam War. And his mother, her face so different from Les' in its shape and coloring, long and narrow and reddish, was not tuned into the dog show at all but spearing little bits of meat out of the sukiyaki left on their plates.

Had he been home?

What the fuck?

* * *

He closed the door to his room. They didn't usually close doors in that house; but it was summer, he had his own air conditioner.

Even with the door shut, light turned off, the room wasn't com-pletely dark. His father kept a bug bulb burning in the front porch lamp whose yellow haze shone into the space of window above his air conditioner.

He jumped into the bed, pulled the covers over him. He felt cold with the air conditioning going so strong; it was right next to his head.

His room had wooden walls. In the semidarkness, they seemed to move far away from him, like trunks in a forest, to even reassume their old wood smell. Some allergy prickled his nose; he rubbed it.

He lay down on his back, his knees up beneath his sheets to form a tent around his lower body. His dick was hard. Just shutting the door was enough to do that.

He pushed his hand below the elastic of his pajamas and touched it, lightly, tentatively, at first; each time it was as if he explored some-thing completely unknown, even something so known.

He had planned to get out one of the Playboy magazines to look at while he masturbated, but now he was in bed, he could not bear to move back into the refrigerated air. Ants crawled inside his thighs, urgency.

He tried to relax. He lay down flat on his back, keeping one hand on his dick; he put the other hand under his head.

Why hadn't she told him right away? Why hadn't she told Mom?

Maybe it really was just money, Duke always after some dough.

He felt his body dip, sway. He felt his dick soften at the idea of money. Then harden again as he thought of paying it for sex.

Christ, what was wrong with his parents? Anyone could see the man was half crazy.

He rubbed himself slowly, trying to think of the Playboy magazines he had hidden away. (Duke had been right about that). He had been looking at a Christmas one this morning. The girl on the cover wore a stocking cap and a red velvet bikini with bits of white rabbit fur everywhere right.

He tried to remember the girl in the red tufted bikini, and, inside that issue, a picture of Raquel Welch in torn-up fur skins.

Shit. (Why hadn't she yelled for help?)

And then there was this other girl, on the inside cover, with shaving cream sprayed all over her privates. Sort of like that Tijuana Brass cover, but a lot more since you could really see things in Playboy.

He tried to conjure up the cracked sidewalks of the swimming pool, Cheryl Bates who Johnny was supposed to be screwing, the way she wore her bikini low down beneath her belly button, the wobble of belly and the hint of crack when you watched her from behind.

Instead there was Duke and Les downstairs, the white cinderblocks, deaf walls.

He kept masturbating. Les was falling over Duke's hand, hanging onto his shoulders, Duke patting her.

He knew this was not right. She was just a child, his sister. But there it was, Les's long hair swaying, he couldn't stop it.

A cannibal chief tore pictures out of a dirty magazine and stuffed them into his mouth. 'I say is that dehydrated stuff any good?' asked one of his wives.

Shit. Shit shit shit shit shit.

He pressed his eyes closed, then open. The ceiling of his wooden room was painted white. He found himself picturing stereotypes of round dark bellies and in their hands, the torn photos of brunettes, blondes, nipples.

He pulled his hand away. He turned over onto his stomach, his full weight pressing his cock, as if he could squash it. The bottom sheet was hot. The air conditioner hummed its constant accordion.

As he turned his head to the side, his eyes caught a small wooden carving, Norwegian, that sat on the table by his bed. A fisherman who had caught the back of his pants with his fishing hook, his face was rounded into an "O" expressing confusion, surprise, embarrassment. His carved cheeks were very red and he wore a green mountaineer's hat.

Idiot. Why did he have such things in his room? Fifteen years old.

He wanted to get up right then and crush it into a hundred thousand pieces.

Why didn't he just do that? Crush it all to hell.

He felt semen dribble out of his cock, and turning the pillow onto its cool side, pushed his face into it. Stupid. Stupid stupid stupid stupid. Turned over onto his side trying to ignore the lingering pressure in his dick, the want of anything.

Why did she have to tell him all this shit? So he could what? Just feel bad for her—

Les
Suburban Maryland
July, 1968

She was pregnant. It seemed as if Duke had something on his finger, something bad. She remembered a joke her mother whispered to her Aunt Grady once about getting pregnant from something on her leg. It must have been something like that.

The worst part was that she would have to tell now. Soon it would begin to show.

Everyday she looked in the mirror to check for changes. Instead of looking at her stomach, she surveyed her bare back. She could see it with ease, not even needing a second mirror.

At first, the skin was flat and smooth. Then the pregnancy began to show itself in the sprouting of vines. The vines reminded her of a plant on their kitchen windowsill, whose green leaves were waxy and veined in yellow. Only the vines growing from her back were much longer than those of the plant in the kitchen, and they were pulled downward by large buds made of clam shells, heavy lotus bud clam shells, hard, ribbed, grey on the outside but with violet petals, yellow stamens, clustered within.

The vines grew in a grid across and up and down her back. Because the vines were so long, the top ones curled and tangled with the lower ones and the clam shells clumped together in odd bunches.

What was hard to believe was how quickly they grew. Overnight.

Overnight? They seemed to lengthen even in the time she looked at herself in the mirror.

They would surely know now–her mother, her dad, Arne. All they had to do is take one look.

Cut them off, she thought. At least then she could wear a Tshirt.

But how could she reach back there? With a scissors? A knife?

But she was afraid of scissors, afraid of a knife.

She imagined a grove of naked stems, dry persistent roots, like when her father pushed the lawn mower over a remnant of bush.

But she feared uprooting the vines even more than cutting them. She was afraid to tug at something embedded in her. And what would that do to the baby?

When she walked away from the mirror, she felt the vines following her, the clam shells thumping against her back.

She thought of tin cans following a newly-weds' car, clanking tin cans and shaving cream and big lipstick kisses.

But the vines did not follow her like that. They only rustled. After all, no matter how hard the shells themselves might be, they hit bare skin.

* * *

Every hour on the hour they had a fifteen minute rest period. It was a time when all the screaming, splashing, marco poloing, stopped and grown-ups, with their strange dry strokes, puffy backs and silken bathing caps, swam slow laps. You had to be over sixteen to stay in the water.

Like the other kids, Les sat along the edge of the pool, waiting for the whistle. A boy with red hair, older than her but clearly below sixteen, slipped silently from the ledge across, and ducked beneath the water, his body an expanded wriggle beneath the blue.

She felt the whole poolside watching him, holding its collective breath till he pulled himself up onto the pool's opposite side, head sleek as an otter, water shimmering down his back. Everyone, in relief and pleasure, readjusted their bottoms, hid their smirks. It was as if they had all fooled the guard.

Then Les felt herself alone again, herself the watched one.

She hadn't talked to Arne all day, but she knew he had been keeping an eye on her, even as he pretended not to.

What had she told him? Why had she said anything?

It was because of the grass. She'd heard him and Jasper talking about it when she'd been hiding in the bushes beside the patio. She hadn't meant to hear, she just had, and then when she went down there, she knew they had done it, the way they looked. It was so crazy, Arne smoking grass, Arne, the math nerd.

She'd wondered whether maybe it meant that he was different from what she'd always thought; that maybe he was normal, human, someone she could actually talk to.

But it was stupid to think that. Because he wasn't any different. He was the same old Arne. And now she had said something to him, something stupid.

Bruce Beebee was at the pool too, Bruce from school. Bruce, who didn't even belong to that swimming pool, Bruce with a streak of white stuff down his nose, a deep tan everywhere else, sitting on a picnic table at the snack bar with his brother. He was not directly looking at her either; yet she felt his looks all the same, and in his looks, she felt this change in herself, a change that showed as much as his thick white streak, only the streak looked almost cool, and she couldn't think of herself as cool, not even this changed self.

She answered his not looking at her by not looking at him, crossing her arms over her chest, keeping her eyes down towards the water.

Arne hulked by Bruce's brother. She had forgotten that they knew each other, and Jasper too, and they were all standing or leaning on the picnic table talking, Jasper eating a frozen Snickers bar, Bruce listening to them, holding his tennis racket between his legs, two palms pressed against the racket part.

She wondered whether Arne was telling them something, telling them what she had said.

He wouldn't–she knew he wouldn't–and yet, with the echo of his telling in her mind, she couldn't stand not looking at them any more, not being looked at in return, and she got up from the side of the pool and walked slowly towards the girls' locker room, feeling in the boys' not-looks the pucker of her bathing suit inside her buttocks, and she hurried her walk a little, though she still aimed for nonchalance, not wanting to reach down and tug the suit loose, not with them not watching.

The locker room was immediately cool. It smelled of wet paint and wet toilet paper and dank chlorinated concrete, all tinged with Coppertone. She sat down on a short blue bench by a wall of wooden cubby holes. The surface of the bench was knobby with repeated paint jobs. She ran her finger over a speckled place that someone had already started to peel.

How could she go back to school in the fall? She hadn't even thought about that part. Her mom might not notice anything, but kids would.

Now two older girls burst in, falling over each other through the bright doorway, the flesh of their stomachs rolling over their bikinis.

'Did you see that?' they laughed, 'what he did?' 'I almost died.'

They laughed themselves to the mirror, which for a moment, they seemed to embrace. They were closer there, their warm baby oil seeping over her. Then the dark-haired girl dug into an open cubby and, finding a tube of lipstick behind some rolled-up cut-offs, coated her lips in ghostly lavender.

The other girl, whose hair was lighter, messed with a brown paper bag folded around a half lemon. Leaning against the mirror, she pulled one side of hair back above her ears and squeezed juice over it, combing as she squeezed and picking at the pulp and seeds that clung to the wet strands.

"Jesus, this stuff is shit; does it look horrible?" she said.

"No more than usual," the dark-haired girl said.

The other scowled.

"Just kidding," the dark-haired one laughed. "Come on, it just looks a little wet; that's all."

They re-tied each other's bikini tops. As one tied, the other looked at herself in the mirror, trying out a selection of smiles. Beneath the smiles, the floating triangles of cloth re-centered themselves.

Les looked down at the bench, conscious of her own breasts. Nothing like these girls, but different from what they had been, no longer a simple ribcage of breath.

Could she tell them? It would be like telling her friends, only they weren't her friends, so it would be better. She would never have to talk to them again.

"This really weird thing happened to me–" she could say.

She tried to imagine them leaning into her like they leaned into the mirror.

'Some people might think it was cool,' she could say.

Leaning into her, listening to her, not even noticing after a bit that she was actually one of the younger kids.

She would like that.

Arne went home early with Jasper. She could have gone too; they asked her; Arne asked her for them, but she said no, she'd wait for their mom.

Bruce from her school left too, waving at her just before he left. She grudgingly waved back.

She waited for her mother at the edge of the swimming pool's parking lot, sitting on a dark brown log that looked like a fallen telephone pole. She pressed her bare feet into the gravel, curling her toes around small rows of stones as if to gather foot-fulls.

Normally, it made her furious to wait for her mom. It wasn't that she was impatient. It was just that her mother was always late.

She couldn't feel that anger now. She could only find fear–fear that the next time she saw her mom, all would be changed, that her mother would pick her up with red eyes, a face lined with disappointment.

But her mother was just late, she told herself. It wasn't anything special.

She began to count slowly. One, two, three, four, five.

If she doesn't come by ten, si–ix, se—v—en, se—v–en mississippi.

If she doesn't come by twenty.

The pool was on a back road. Cars rarely passed. Each time she heard one coming, she slowed her count more to give her mom a chance to make it by the lower number.

A big old white whale with a pink top, a black square boxy kind. A few minutes later a robin's egg blue VW bug. A maroon station wagon with wood panels on the side.

Every once in a while, some one else left the pool. Wrapped in towel or towel dress. "Hi." "Bye." "You need a ride?" "No thanks."

She thought again about Bruce, Bruce from her class. They had done flag duty together all year long, both school patrols. She remembered the day after Bobby Kennedy had died. How mad she had been at Bruce, Bruce who had played desk football while they were waiting for news about Bobby; Bruce who had wanted to watch cartoons.

He had waited for her that next morning outside the front door of the school, just past the bulletin board that, even in June, still sported cherries for George Washington's birthday.

"You're late," he had said.

Bruce had a narrow tan face, with a mouth that always twisted into a crescent of sneer. His hair was wavy and short and so closely matched his face in color that his forehead seemed to curl into it.

They knew the routine well, unfolding the triangle they had folded the flag into the afternoon before, hooking the side with the holes into the gold metal hooks on the rope attached to the flag pole. Bruce usually did the hooking, while she held the opposite side.

But when she looked at Bruce that morning, the sneering waves of hair, gaze, mouth, something insistent took hold of her and she'd said, "I want to try hooking it."

"You did that already," he'd said.

"Just once. You do it all the time and I only did it once."

He had paused, but then, surprisingly, had handed over the side with the holes. "Okay, but just this time. And be careful."

She had felt like saying, 'you be careful.' She had felt like saying, outraged, 'just this time!'

Instead, she quietly took hold of the white canvas border and began squeezing the hooks into the holes.

"You got to squeeze really hard," he said. "Here, you want me to do it?"

"I've got it," she said, squeezing so hard she pinched her finger. But then, as she moved down to the bottom hook, she glanced towards Bruce—

"Bruce, you're dropping it!"

"Dammit!" He grabbed the end up quickly; he bunched the flag all together. "You've got to *hold* it," she said.

"I *was* holding it. You should've let me hook it."

"It's not fair you always getting to hook it."

There was more to argue, only then, looking up to the window of the principal's office, they both had just shut up.

"I don't think she saw anything," Bruce whispered.

"Should we tell her? It's supposed to be burned."

"Just hook it and pull it up. Look, you want me to do it?"

"They don't even throw away flags; they're supposed to be burned."

"It's not like we dropped it in the mud," Bruce said, and then, quietly, carefully, they towed the rope that raised the flag up its line.

She remembered looking up to it, as she stared now across the swimming pool parking lot.

If only Duke had let her talk to him before he left. If only they had promised not to tell.

She shivered against the stillness of the chrome fenders, against the weight of the trees across the way, so heavy with heat and silence.

Then opened up *Gone With the Wind.* Atlanta had just been burned and Scarlett was making the long trek back to Tara with Prissy screaming in the background, Melanie conked out.

She shut the book abruptly. She didn't like that part. She didn't like any of the parts with slaves in them, the "darkies." Those parts were all so strange now. Her mother said she didn't even know how they could let the movie out again. Though when she said that, she also acted like they *should* let the movie out again.

She didn't like to think about it. Still, opened the book again, more towards the end.

This was Rhett and Scarlett, yes, the night of their big fight—"drink it, I say," said Rhett.

Her dad's white VW station wagon pulled up in a crush of gravel. She hadn't heard it coming and started. He leaned over to the passengers' side to push open the door.

"Hey Les," he smiled, waving at her with his head.

She closed the book, moved slowly towards the car. "I thought Mom was coming."

"She was, but then Wainwright called, you know how it is, and I'd gotten off early today so I thought, hey, a chance to go get Les." He smiled.

As if he didn't pick her up every day of her life, Les thought. She had wanted her mother.

"Here, let me shut the door for you," he said, and before she knew it, he was tugging at his seat belt, and (grunting lightly) pushing himself up and out of the seat to get out, coming around to her side of the car.

"Watch out for fingers," he said as he took hold of the door. But still he himself made sure that her hands were in her lap, then slammed the door hard, pressing the thumb part of the handle in and out to make sure it was locked. He looked back and forth and down to the ground quickly to check that she hadn't forgotten anything, and hustled back to his side of the car again, scrunched into his seat, and shifting heavily, squealed the car into motion.

All of this irritated her incredibly. Then the irritation made her feel guilty. Because she knew he was trying to be nice; that, in fact, he *was* being nice.

He drove the small car as if his body were part of the engine, tilting as he shifted in what seemed a strategic fashion, something to add or take away from the momentum

"So how are you, baby boop?" he said, relaxing and turning to her. "Did you wait long?"

"Well," she said, complainingly.

"I'm sorry. You know how Mom is. Someone calls at exactly the wrong time and then she just gets preoccupied."

"She has a clock."

He sighed. He frowned. "I know. But you can't be too hard on her, rushing around all the time here and there. Not even a minute to rest, take a breath," he grumbled. "Anyway, I'm glad I was home. I don't get a chance to just be with you very often. Gee." He looked over to her, smiling his shiny-headed, shiny-glassed, shiny-toothed smile.

A blacktop road stretched ahead, and around them a heavy girdle of green. The sunroof was open and a warm draft blew down upon her, a rippling scarf. She shut her eyes, trying to put herself back into *Gone with the Wind*. Rhett would be picking up Scarlett soon, melting her with kisses, carrying her up the stairs: "this is one night there are not going to be two men in my bed."

Rhett was like Duke, Duke like Clark Gable. She felt a little bad that she had never really liked Rhett that much. It was Ashley she had always loved, quiet, noble, blonde. Ashley whom she was even named for in a way, Leslie Howard.

But now, she felt she should really try to like Rhett more, to prefer Rhett.

"I opened the sunroof for you," her dad said. "Is that okay?"

"Sure," she said. "Thank you, Daddy."

Leaning her head into the warm draft from the sunroof, she went back to the scene from the book, Rhett/Duke, and became intensely conscious of her breasts, this feeling of life there. The feeling almost hurt. She thought of the girls in the locker room, the little triangles of bikini top, the soft pillows of flesh. But then Duke came again too, Duke/Rhett, with large rough hands, flattening, pressing her down.

She felt cold, sick. She shifted in her seat and cupped her hands over her eyes to focus them into the car.

Her father's car had recently been hit in the back by a lumber truck. Not his fault, according to him–he had to stop suddenly and couldn't get away from it. But after the car was fixed, he had taped up a variety of small messages written on white adhesive tape along the dashboard and glove compartment. (The driver's side of the dash was too crowded with dials to hold any.)

She concentrated on these. "Keep Vigilance." That was the main one. He had written that on almost every tape, and then, scrawled above and below: "Drive Slowly." "Look Behind." "Use Caution at all Times." "WATCH OUT FOR BIG TRUCKS".

The signs made Arne mad. 'They're too far away for you to read,' he complained. 'All they do is scare the passengers.'

Les liked them. "Keep Vigilance" especially. It was just such a cool word. Though also a little word. Vigilance wasn't a word she ever heard her father use and here he had it taped up three times.

"Hey Les, how about going to that new Roy Rodgers place, huh? Are you hungry? Arne's up at the Lowells and, Mom–well, you know, she's got all her stuff going on still."

She wanted to see her mom. She wanted to lie down in her mother's air-conditioned bed and watch her type up her paper, listen to her talk to Mona Wainwright if nothing else.

She just wanted to be there, guard her mom.

"I don't have my shoes."

"I was afraid of that, see, so I grabbed a pair. Mom said they were yours" he gestured with his head. "Back there–"

A pair of scuffed blue sneakers hunkered down on the back seat.

Darn it. But he was right. Without Arne there would be nothing much at home, no regular dinner.

"Okay," she said.

He smiled, straightening up as his foot deepened into the accelerator.

"Yeah," he said. "They're pretty good there. They have ice cream too."

She wanted to shout, 'I don't care about things like that—ice cream. Don't you get it, Dad? I don't care about things like that.'

"Great," she said.

They drove through an area with more houses, the great big Methodist church, the shacks of Saint Barnabas Road, and then slowly, the gas stations, florist, seven eleven, new jr. hot shoppes

She looked at her father, his eager bald profile, moist tan skin. Suddenly his normally soft face turned into an angry mask, grimacing and cursing at a car that cut him off

Then changing back, "I'm sorry. I know I shouldn't get so mad at the jokers"

The way he changed, the way he changed back–though she knew her father, that he loved her certainly, that he loved her more than anything– Still, she wished he wouldn't get mad like that.

* * *

The Roy Rodgers had red lights inside big wagon wheel chandeliers and red and white checked curtains lining the walls, curtains everywhere except for the actual windows which were wide and clear. Cars coming and going and a new building and parking lot being built across the street. A frame of a hat out in front of the new building; it looked like it was going to be an Arby's.

They each got roast beef sandwiches. That was one nice thing about going with her dad. Her mom always wanted to get one thing and split it–chicken usually–which she would carefully peel, pulling off all the skin and fried bits, before she gave you your half. But with her dad, you could get whatever you wanted, and everyone got their own.

Her dad ate hungrily, flattening the thick roast beef sandwich between his two fists. She was hungry too, but didn't want to join in with such gusto. She unwrapped her sandwich slowly, with deliberate delicacy.

"Gee this is nice," he smiled. "Just to be with Leslie." He readjusted his glasses with one hand and picked up his sandwich with the other. "I like the way they say 'happy trails, pardner.'" He laughed. "They really do say it too. Every time you go by. Even when I went back for that danged tea."

"It's kind of silly," she said.

"So, I guess we'll be going out to Minnesota next week to see Grandma."

Her heart caught in her throat. "Minnesota? I thought we weren't going."

"Well, we weren't with Mom's course and everything. I thought it was too dang much. But she's almost done now and she wants to go."

"Who's out there?"

"I don't know. Grady has been, but I think Mom said she'll have gone back by the time we get there." He pushed his glasses higher up his nose, thinking. "Yeah, that's right. That's another reason she wants to go now, so Grandma won't be by herself."

"Duke's not there?"

"Oh, *he* might be, I don't know." Her dad chuckled. "You know how he is. It's not like he tells anyone his plans." He laughed louder. "But he might stop by. Even Minnesota's golf can't be too bad in the middle of summer."

Smiling, he looked down at the table, his empty wrapper, picked up a bit of a crumb, and put it quickly quickly between his lips; they shone like the top of a burger bun.

She still had quite a bit left. She tried to take another bite, the roast beef too cold, too slippery.

Her dad sighed. He looked over his glasses at a waitress in cowboy hat and short skirt who was carrying a tray of food to a counter for an older woman. He waited for the waitress to set the woman up, peering over his glasses. Then –Les could see the idea twirling around in his head as the waitress came back up the aisle, chuckling and face reddening, "Howdy pardner," he blurted out.

After that, he quickly withdrew both into his own pleasure and embarrassment, pulling his nose lightly, drinking his ice tea.

"Dad," she groaned.

He crumpled up his sandwich wrapper. "Oh well," he sighed. "I guess I shouldn't do that."

"No, you shouldn't," she said. She looked out the window to the incipient highway, and across, at the huge bare hat frame, the fast food restaurant to come.

"So, you think Duke might be there?"

He shrugged. "I don't know, Baby. I wouldn't mind seeing him though. I felt awful to miss him when he was here. I like Duke. You know how he always makes me laugh."

The wooden walls of the restaurant seemed too close. She had to do something, go somewhere. Not home though. She tried to think. She tried to come up with something.

"Daddy, you remember–"

"Huh?"

"You remember that time we went to Hecht's to look for my little purse—I lost it, remember? And then when I went to the lost and found, they didn't have that purse, but they had an old one I'd lost, one I'd lost a few years before, an old black patent leather Sunday school purse, remember?"

"Oh yeah," he said, pulling his nose. "And it still had those funny green stamps they gave out at Sunday school in it too. Imagine that? That was so funny." He smiled, his round face widening.

It wasn't what she had wanted to say.

Except that it gave her an idea.

"Daddy, could we go to Hecht's right now? Would you mind?"

"Right now?"

"Yeah, I need to get something; I almost forgot."

He scowled down at his watch. "Right now?" Then stared up into the air, as if figuring out a math problem. "Sure, well, I guess so, "he said. "They should be open at least another hour."

"Mom won't care if we're late."

"No."

She got up quickly, he with more reluctance. "You're sure you don't want any ice cream?"

In the department store, she looked at the rack of training bra boxes from a distance, trying to keep her father from understanding what she was looking at, trying to keep anyone from understanding. It was always possible that a friend from school would pop by, though she didn't think that was too likely. Nighttime shopping wasn't something her friends did. When your mother worked, you were used to doing all kinds of things at night, but most of their mothers stayed at home.

It wasn't hard to fool her dad. He was used to not paying attention to anything in a department store. His habit, developed from the marathon shopping expeditions Ingrid favored, was to find a chair in a quiet but not too remote spot (he didn't want to be accused of hiding) and to either read the paperback he carried in his back pocket, usually something involving spies and swastikas, or to jot down numbers, letters, and little squiggly lines.

There was a rack of bathing suits for sale across from the boxes of training bras, the little-pink-girl-covered cartons. She kept looking to her sides to make sure no one watched her. Every once in a while, she even swiped a bathing suit along the round metal rod next to her to make it seem as if she were shopping for one of those.

Her father did look up from his book to smile and wave, his face filled with an exaggerated glow of recognition, but he wasn't really paying attention.

At last, she stepped directly to the bra rack. The little signs said 30, 32, 34. She knew 36 meant something. She'd heard that often enough. 36-24-36. The ideal numbers for a woman. Though Scarlett was supposed to have a seventeen inch waist. Crazy. Course people had stays back then

The Hawkinsons all had good waistlines, good busts, so her mother said, but were a little big in the hips.

She pictured her mother's hips. They were like a wide flat board in her girdle, lumpy without, then more like a cushion. Her father looked up and smiled at her again.

The sales woman, a small older lady, whose pointed nose, yellowed skin, clipped hair, reminded Les of a terrier, asked if she could help.

Go away. Leave me alone.

"I'm just looking for a—" Les said, crossing her arms over the part of the T-shirt that covered her chest. She could feel the terrier softly sniffing her there, assessing–

"You can try one on" the woman said, nodding towards the rack, "as long as you don't get the boxes all mixed up"

Les grabbed a couple of boxes, paying no attention to the numbered sizes.

"Little Miss" one brand was called.

The dressing room smelled of gray carpeting. Les pulled the curtain closed, as tight as it would go. But when it closed on one side, it opened on the other. Finally, holding the boxes under one arm, she tugged each side of the curtain gently gently, trying for maximum coverage. In the women's dressing rooms they had wooden screens, she thought, not these stupid curtains.

It felt so strange to be in a dressing room by herself. This was her mother's domain. The only other times Les had been in one by herself, she had been waiting, back up to the mirror with a book or a bag of candy, while her mother was outside, at the big three-sided mirrors surveying herself. You couldn't get a good view in those dressing room mirrors, she always said.

Les tried not to look at herself, but at the boxes. She jumbled one bra out. It wasn't like one of her mother's at all. It was made of a thick soft cloth. There was no rubber, no cup of lace; well, there was a trim of lace, pink bow in the center. The whole thing was teeny.

She took off her T-shirt and peeled down her bathing suit. She tried not to look at her breasts bare, though it was a hard not to see them, the mirror so close. The skin looked starkly white, too smooth in comparison to her tanned sun-sloughed limbs.

She approached the bra as she had seen her mother do, back to front to snap it, then twisted it around the right way. The material cupped over her chest like nothing.

It was odd to have the bra on top, the slick rind of her bathing suit on the bottom. She put her T-shirt over it and, standing very straight, looked for a hint of the outline.

Then, fearful that if the terrier stuck her head in she would think she was trying to steal something, she hurried off her shirt, swished the bra around, unsnapped it.

She pulled up her suit, put on her shirt, and stuffed the bra, as limp and white as a diaper, back into the right box.

It was dark when they left the store. Les was glad of it, for she felt a great giddiness, her face wild with smiling.

Her father had looked startled when she called him to the register to pay for it, but he had said nothing except to find out the exact price. Even now he said little, only putting his hand on her arm as they walked through the parking lot to protect her from passing cars. But he whispered it to her mother when they got home.

"You really want to get into all of that?" Ingrid asked laughing. "I'd think you'd want to put it off until you really had to"

Les's excitement cracked into panic–where was Arne?

"Mo-om."

She tried to keep her face smooth as she went past Arne's open door. His room was empty. Good. She felt as if she would kill him if he had been there laughing at her.

She rushed the bag with the bra in it into her room. She half shut her door and stuck the box into a never-used drawer of her wooden vanity, one of her own secret drawers. She got out her pjs and put them on, leaving her clothes, her swimsuit, in loops shaped by her ankles, on the floor.

Her breath caught itself again and again as if in a squashed game of tag. Her breasts felt huge right now, swollen with recaptured feeling, a swallowed flag. She was glad she'd bought the bra. She did too need it.

She took her copy of *Gone with the Wind* to her bed but she didn't really want it anymore. Got up and went to the old green Norwegian book shelf that stood in the corner of her room, squeezing out from the tight row of books, the diary of Anne Frank. She took it quickly to her bed where she lay on her side facing the wall.

She cried as she read. Her tears seemed to turn the slick green bedspread into something slimy.

"Les, are you okay?" her mom said, poking through the half closed door.

She wiped her face again quickly. "I was just looking through *Anne Frank*," she said.

"Oh dear," her mother said, sitting down next to her.

Les rubbed her face again. Her mother took her hair in her hands, pulling it lightly from her forehead and the back of her neck. Les tried to relax into her mother's hands.

But then her mother sighed, let go of her hair, and leaned over for the book, which she took on her own lap after a moment, reading here and there, shuddering.

"She really was a wonderful writer, wasn't she?" she said. "It wasn't just these terrible experiences, but her philosophy"

Her mother's body smelled of hand lotion. Les leaned into it. She loved that smell, but especially now, the way it made her conscious of the chlorine that embedded her own skin.

Maybe she should just tell her. Her mother, who knew so much. Maybe she should just tell her, so her mom could say 'look, don't worry about it.' Maybe she would understand the whole thing, groan, but chuckle too, say, 'look, that's how men are.'

Her mom got up and began straightening the room, restacking the books on her vanity, picking her bathing suit, T-shirt and shorts from the floor, folding them.

"You know it's fine if you want to start wearing a bra, sweetie. I just wasn't expecting you'd go out and get it yourself."

Les nodded. "I'm sorry," she said.

"No, it's fine. It's great, if that's what you want." She put the bathing suit, shorts and shirt on the vanity. "Can I see it?"

Les padded over to the vanity drawer. She didn't really want her mother to see where she had hid it, but pulled it out, handed her the bag, then climbed back into bed.

Her mom took the box out of the bag with the hands of an experienced shopper. Unfolded the bra (Les felt her cheeks burning), smiled, then refolded it, patting the material as if it were a little animal. "It's nice and soft, that's good. If you don't really need one, at least it's something comfortable."

Les looked down at her books; Anne Frank's dark eyes stared up at her, serious, hopeful.

"Goodnight sweetie," her mother said. "Do you want me to turn off the light?"

"No, that's okay."

After her mother left, Les put the books beside her pillow, and thought about turning off the light. But she felt now that she could not get up, that there was too much blocking her.

If only she could talk to him. If only she could get him to promise.

But how could she talk to him? How could she call? How could she say the words even if she could call.

She couldn't call, she couldn't *say* the words, but she could write them, she thought. She'd have to send the letter to Minnesota, but her grandma went down town to pick up the mail every single day. There were letters for Duke all the time.

She got a blue spiral notebook from her vanity, a pen, and instead of turning off the light, half shut the door again.

But maybe writing was too dangerous. Maybe writing wouldn't work. She pictured him opening up the envelope. If it *was* him.

But Grandma wouldn't open Duke's mail.

It still might make him mad. She pictured him tearing the envelope open, his face grizzled and impatient, his fingers, holding a cigar, thick like pale sausages

He might tear the envelope so deeply that the letter would get torn too. He might have to piece it together to read it.

De ar Uncle Duke,
    I promise not to
te   ll anybody.
De ar Uncle Duke,
    I promise I have not
to   ld.

But she had told somebody.

She made big x's across the page.

She'd promised not to tell anyone and then she'd gone and told Arne. She'd forgotten about Arne.

What had she said? She couldn't think, couldn't remember.

Big X's that she outlined in loopy blocks like Peter Max.

She wrote Arne's name too and made a big x over it, a big loopy x.

She tore the page out and crumpled it.

She was just about to push the crumpled page down between her bed and the wall when she thought of her mother pulling her bed from the wall to mop up the floor. She did that every once in a while. It would be just like her to uncrumple any piece of paper and look at it.

She got up quickly, lightly, and put the crumpled paper in the bottom pullout drawer of the green Norwegian bookshelf that sat in one corner of her room, then stole back into bed. She lay on her side, propping herself up on an elbow, covering her shoulder with the green slightly slimy comforter. Cold.

But maybe she could write him just a normal letter.

"Dear Duke," she wrote.

No.

She turned the page.

"Dear Uncle Duke," she wrote.

"How are you? I am fine."

What else?

"I hope that your malaria's not acting up?"

She could say that.

She could say anything, she realized, because she wasn't going to send this letter either, not unless she sent it the way she sent a letter to Doogie after he died, placing it in the "D" volume of her Junior Britannica—D for Doogie, D of dachshund—hoping for transmission to some kind of D-dog heaven.

She drew a little heart in the margin of the page. This is what the girls did in school. Cool girls. It felt funny to be doing it in the summer.

Little curly-q hearts, the bottom points slightly twisted. Little initialed hearts. Little hearts with arrows through them.

And if someone really liked you, some boy, he gave you a necklace with a heart on it, only the heart had a piece cut out, a piece in the shape of key, which the boy was supposed to keep for himself. So that he held the key to your heart.

Or maybe it was the opposite, he'd give you the key, the girl.

* * *

Her teeth were crumbling. When she swallowed, she tasted them in her mouth, the front ones especially, a chalky calcified dust.

At first, she told her mother that she was losing a filling. But when she heard her on the phone to the dentist, she couldn't keep it inside any more and told her the real problem, that her teeth were crumbling. She was very upset, imagining how she would look with no teeth, with bits and pieces of teeth. Every time she swallowed, her tongue clogged with the calcified gravel.

The dentist came to their house. He lay her down on the couch to examine her mouth, then asked to see the rough stuff she kept feeling on her tongue. She licked some out into her hand.

There were tiny sea shells, small scallops, pointed conches, those tiny speckled earlobes that crowd the sand where the surf breaks.

No problem with her teeth, the dentist said. The shells just came from sand she had been eating earlier.

"Next time you should be sure to sift that sand, wash it," the dentist said. Her mother nodded sternly. "If you don't want to keep spitting it up."

She woke in pain. She put her finger in her mouth to feel her teeth, but it wasn't her teeth that bothered her. Her throat held a sharp hard lump, like a swallowed ice cube.

She realized, as if for the first time, that it wasn't Duke she had to worry about–it was Arne, Arne, goddamn him.

If only she hadn't told him. What did she have to go and tell him for?

If she hadn't told him, they could just forget about all this–she and Duke. They would never have to talk of it again.

Her mom wouldn't have to know, her dad, Grady, Jasper, none of them.

She turned over to her side to go back to sleep, but, as she shut her eyes, she saw the sea shells in her hand, felt again that terrible crumbling.

She got up slowly. She was afraid to take a step. It was as if she might step upon the cracked shells, only they would be sharp now, sharp shards.

She would have liked to have her dad there in the hall, waiting for her, shepherding her, but she didn't want to call him. If he had just happened to be getting up to go to the bathroom, it would have been okay, but she could not be that little pink girl, calling girl–

She held her breath and leapt from the bed, aiming to land as far away from it as possible, far where nothing could grab her, then walked quickly across her floor, the hall, and into her parents' room, where she slowed down, walking on the softest tiptoe she could manage. She felt now that she shouldn't be there without having called her dad first, as if she were sneaking in without that. She felt like a spy, a soldier, maybe even a thief. As if she could be caught, punished for sneaking in. And it was so cold there, the air conditioner like a sentence.

* * *

She went into Arne's room the next morning early while her mom was drinking coffee in the kitchen, her dad already off to work. She moved quickly, sure for a couple of moments of what she was going to say.

He was sitting cross-legged on his bed looking at a red paperback called Mathematic Probability with a big graph on the cover. He was still in his pajamas and, as was his way in the early morning, he rubbed his nose incessantly.

Seeing him alone made her skin tingle, this thing in her chest sway around, crazed ghost. She felt herself downstairs in the back room.

She felt Duke next to her, the rough warm brush of his cheeks against her bare arms, the rubbed calloused hands around her waist as they placed her feet onto the floor. 'How do you like my waist?'

The brown wood walls of her brother's room made it dark–what with the air conditioner in the only window and small what with him sitting there, with his long body, big head, reddened nose. The place was even more crowded by this picture she kept seeing of herself and Duke rattling around like beebees in the barrel of a gun, herself and Duke in her head.

In Dime, Minnesota where her grandmother lived, there was a wonderful green park. If Duke was there, he would walk with her to that park. There were dark red swings and an obstacle course and the shell of an old bandstand you could tap dance on a stage, even sing.

She tried to think of dancing on that abandoned stage and shut the door lightly behind her, darkening the room even more. Arne looked up.

"You know that thing I told you, that silly thing about Duke, I don't know why I said that." She felt her face reddening. "I don't even know what I said. Except that it was idiotic."

She tried to read his expression, but his nose was red, his eyes caught in the shadowy glare of his glasses.

"Honest," she went on. "You guys were acting so big with all that— well, you know what you had. And I was mad because–well, you know, you shouldn't really do stuff like that, Arne."

"What are you talking about? That girl stuff? Les, I told you that was just ridiculous."

"Not that, Arne. You know what I mean."

"I know what?"

"That stuff Jasper brought."

An instant of alarm, wonder, fear spread over his face and then morphed to sullen anger. "What the fuck are you talking about?"

She bit her lip. "I was hiding and, well, I meant it as a joke. I was going to run out and scare you, and then you two started talking, I didn't know what to do–"

"God, you're a creep, spying on us–"

"I wasn't spying on you, I mean, well, I was–but it was joke. But then when Jasper started talking about–well, you know, then I just couldn't just run out anymore."

"Jasper talking about what?"

"Do you really want me to say it?" she whispered, dashing a look over her shoulder.

"Jerk."

"Arne–I didn't say I was going to tell Mom. I mean, I don't think you should be doing it, but I'm not going to tell."

"Go to hell."

"You shouldn't talk like that to me. I'm just trying to be nice."

"The only nice thing you could do is mind your own business."

"Oh come on, don't be such a–boy. I told you I wouldn't tell and I won't. Not if there's not a reason anyway."

His stare was a cloud; the room night, the wooden walls a forbidden forest.

"What a jerk," he said.

Her face was so hot. He must see it even in the dark. Still, she tried to stare him down.

But he wasn't looking at her. He was leafing through his book again, studying the laws of probability.

"Go away," he said from the pages. "Just leave me alone, jerk."

They didn't speak for the rest of the day. Les went to summer school with her mom. It was okay when the kids were there. She sat in the reading groups, watching them move their fingers along the lines of words like grubby little snails along a slime trail. She helped her mother too, walking among the desks to pass out papers, find stray books. The kids liked her and she felt a bit like a princess among them, the helpful sweet princess, the Florence Nightingale of princesses.

When the kids left, she got very worried. She had to get home. She had to see Arne again. She felt certain suddenly that she had made everything worse. Had she made everything worse? Maybe she should have saved the grass.

She erased and washed the blackboards; she swiped a vinegary sponge over the desks; she tried to concentrate on her tenth reading of *Gone With The Wind.*

Her mother told her, absentmindedly, what a great help she was. She felt like her mother was just saying that to get her to wait patiently. Yet she was afraid to complain too, afraid to risk the 'great help', to be anything that might be even remotely different from how she had always been, even if it was not, in fact, how she had always been. She couldn't be sure anymore.

Her mother talked to Mrs. Batchelor, also known as Wilma, a teacher from down the hall, about how stupid her own course was, the one she was taking at the University: "before I began this course I thought I knew something about statistics, I could have told you something about statistics," she said, "and now, I'm so confused by all their talk, but if I can just get through the exam–"

Les went over to stand next to her mother. Her mother put one arm around her but did not slow her talking. Les, swaying slightly, looked down at her sneakers. The rubber tread had worn away on the sides. Her legs grew out of them like stalks, dry tan stalks, their surface sprinkled with dust.

She slipped away from her mother's side and strayed to the row of children's desks, rehearsing different phrases in her mind. 'Please mom I just can't breathe.' 'Can't we just go somewhere and breathe?' 'Please mom I have to get out of here.'

She lay down on top of the desks. Although she looked at her mother and Mrs. Batchelor, her vision was blurred by the bright yellow of the wood, the yellowness only giving way to deep gouges of pencil. She turned onto her back, so that she wouldn't have to see the marks any more and looked instead at the spackled ceiling.

Her mother walked Mrs. Batchelor out into the hallway, still talking. Then, "well, I'll let you go," she said and stepped back into the classroom.

"Oh sweetie, are you that tired?" her mom said, looking at her directly for a moment. "I'll just be a couple of minutes more."

"Mom, come on."

"Les, honestly, just a few minutes, Sweetie. Look, you want to go down to the faculty room and get a diet soda?"

Les turned onto her stomach. Her hips felt hard against the desk. Were her hips harder than the desk? She didn't think so. She could imagine her hips splintering, the desks had lasted forever.

If Duke wanted to, he could put her over his legs and splinter her hips, he could break her right in two.

She imagined him spanking her, his hand big enough to cover her whole backside.

Now that would get to her mother. Her mom always talked about how she had never spanked her or Arne, had never needed too.

Les turned back on her side to watch her.

Her mother, forgetting her offer of a diet soda, looked through stacks of papers in a cupboard behind her big teacher's desk.

She curled her legs into herself; she put her arms about her knees. She imagined turning herself inside out, her whole being becoming a wet pink tongue and on that tongue, just at the place where her bottom was–well, her front–would be some sign, something her mother would see. Not a statistic, or if it was, the old kind of statistic, the kind her mom understood.

'Look Mom,' she would say.

"Aha," her mom said. Les's body jolted against the desk, bruising the knob of her pelvis, side of knee.

"I got it—great," her mom went on, wiping her bangs out of her face, but still looking intently at the paper. "Great. What a mess to have to do all that over again–"

She read the paper silently, sometimes moving her lips.

"Great," she said again, walking brightly towards the door. "Let me go tell Wilma."

She looked down at the paper as she walked, breaking her stride every few steps to give the page her fuller attention. Les could hear her shoes down the hall, clack clack clack, pause, clack clack.

Les put her head in her arms. She should have tried to be nice to Arne, not make him mad. Why hadn't she been nice?

* * *

That night she and Arne were alone together, her dad out at a special scientists' dinner, her mother at her night class. Arne watched television, scooping up spoons of a half cantaloupe he held in his lap.

She tried to tell what he was thinking. But she couldn't. He wouldn't look at her. He just sat on the big soft chair, watching TV, scratching his great big ankle, jerking his bangs off his forehead, eating cantaloupe.

She hated him. She wanted to bang him with something. She wanted to take the cantaloupe and smoosh it into his face.

But that wasn't going to work. She had to get things straight now. She had to be nice.

She tried to force herself to think of times when she had felt close to him. Once when she was little she ate nearly a whole bottle of Chocks while her mom talked on the phone and Arne had taken her by the hand into her mother, holding the bottle of Chocks in the other hand.

Once in Minnesota, they'd dug a hole all day long, the earth so dank and black, trying to get to China, and finally they'd struck oil they thought, black liquid oozing up from their shovel. When it turned out to be the pipe, Arne had never said it was her fault.

And when Doogie had died, she still remembered Arne's eyes, angry and red rimmed, though Doogie had really been hers.

Now it was the Monkees coming on, their manicured haircuts not blowing in the wind as they hey hey hey heyed outside of car windows and around merry-go-rounds, big leaning heys. She felt herself getting excited. She loved the Monkees. They were silly, but so cute.

But Arne quickly leaned forward; he was so tall he didn't have to get out of the chair and changed the channel to the opening sequence of "The Avengers", the English man on it tipping a black hat into a rose, the English woman's leg pressed to the screen.

He had promised to let her watch the Monkees the week before, one of their endless television tradeoffs.

She wanted to say something.

But there he was, his big foot crossed over his leg, his cantaloupe in his lap, just daring her to try.

The English woman raised her penciled eyebrow, smiled her lipsticked lips, glided her manicured hand over her fishnet stocking.

Arne readjusted his body, putting one foot higher on the opposite thigh, and directed the cantaloupe spoon straight into his mouth without even looking at it.

She thought of standing up in front of the screen. She thought of just waltzing up and changing the channel.

She slipped through the tight space behind his chair to go over to the big new air conditioner. Arne had it turned up high despite its water problem. She dipped water out of the air conditioner's rusted bottom with the long serving spoon her mother left on the stereo just below the window, and emptied the water into the big mixing bowl that was also left there. The English man snared something with his umbrella handle and the English woman said "right-ho", her English accent like a joke.

She dipped with great absorption, trying not to hear the English people, to just get the spoon to the bowl, spoon to bowl, without letting a single drop of that crusted water fall on the stereo, not even onto the towel that lay on top of the stereo, dipping until the bottom of the air conditioner was almost empty, bowl full. This took some time. Even the commercials were over now, even the second commercials. She suddenly realized that she was absolutely chilled.

She slipped back behind Arne's chair and went out to the kitchen. God, she hated him. Boy. Stupid boy. Turning that thing up so high when it dripped.

She sat down on one of the yellow wooden chairs upon the large plastic flower cushions, her mom's attempt at "mod," shivered. The new bra, which she had put on because her mother was going out, felt tight, a hand clapped over a mouth, only it was her chest.

She thought of going to bed, getting under a blanket, taking off the bra, everything, maybe even getting into her mom's bed, getting out *Gone With the Wind.*

"A silly little millimeter longer 101," the TV sang out.

Oh, but she was cold. She thought of turning off the air conditioner, but that was nearly as bad as changing the channel. Arne wouldn't like that. Instead, she went to the stove. She turned on the burners, all four of them. Sometimes in Minnesota on a cold morning, her grandma turned on the oven to heat up the kitchen. She held out her hands to the black coils, waiting for their warmth to start radiating.

She was hungry too. Her dad had made them a quick dinner before he left, blackened hamburgers and frozen corn–he was a terrible dinner cook; she hadn't eaten much.

Then she had an idea. It was one of the sudden great kind that deserve a light bulb overhead. If she were hungry, Arne would be starving! If she made something for him, they could talk.

She hiked herself up onto the formica counter to investigate the high pine cupboards next to the warm stove.

Plenty of flour, sugar. She jumped down and checked the fridge–eggs. She shook the milk carton.

She had another lightbulb of an idea.

Doughnuts!

Doughnuts would be fantastic. Everyone–she thought specifically of her mother–would say how incredible she was, that she had just gone about making doughnuts, all by herself.

She bent down to a drawer jammed with cookbooks. The other day, her dad had brought some doughnuts back from a church social hour, and her mom had gone on and on about them. There was nothing in the world like fresh homemade doughnuts, she'd said.

She leafed through the recipe book. The burners were red now, nice and warm. She put her bowl on the counter to be near them.

She began measuring out the flour, the sugar, nutmeg, salt, vanilla, baking powder, mixing quietly so as not to alert Arne.

The Monkees *were* pretty stupid, she thought, Arne was right.

And he wasn't so bad. She imagined him in a little while, chomping her doughnuts instead of cantaloupe, both of them talking, his knowing then that it had been nothing, nothing. Watching something good.

She took constant licks as she stirred, rubbing her finger along the side of the bowl or along the back of the spoon. The raw creamy sweetness was irresistible.

'You'll be full by the time they're cooked,' she heard in her head. But she didn't really want the doughnuts when they were cooked. It was this she loved, the cold sweet glop, the secret spoonfuls, the part no one else could measure.

Hot next to the burners, she moved to the farther edge of the counter, by the dish rack, reading the directions part of the recipe.

"Drop in ringlets in a vat of hot fat."

Oh no. She'd forgotten that about doughnuts.

She looked through all the recipes. They were all the same. "A pot of hard lard," "boiling oil".

But that was too hard; she couldn't do all that.

Boiling oil? How could she talk to Arne now?

She sat down with the cookbook on the floor. She looked up to the clock. If her mom came back with all that batter sitting there–

It was a cookbook from her grandmother's church in Minnesota. The recipes were all donated by people, town's women, and had really funny names. Millie's sour milk cake. Yankee Doodle Dandy Cake. Mabels' Sunday Best. Helgerson's Jello Cake. Starlight Surprise.

Ginny's French Crepes.

Crepes. Pancakes. She could just make them into pancakes. She went over the list of ingredients. They'd work as pancakes, sure.

Arne loved pancakes. She would even heat up the syrup for him. She would use that little pitcher, the dark one.

She got up and stirred the batter again, lifting the spoon high above the bowl to test the runniness.

The electric burners were really going now, bright red. She stretched out her hands towards them, pulled them back quickly. She turned three of them off.

Still, she felt happy. It was all going to be okay.

She got out a frying pan from the drawer below the oven and put it on the burner closest to the counter. The burner was so hot, the pan gurgled, skidding across the red ring. Her heart jimmied her throat, but she made herself grab the handle, stopping it.

She felt worried now about cooking on the stove. She was more used to the oven.

But what are you going to do with all this batter?

It was *Get Smart* now, that familiar clip-clopping of horns. Had he changed the channel? Or was *The Avengers* over? She peered out the kitchen door. She loved *Get Smart*. Agent Smart, Maxwell Smart, swishing around so importantly as a door slammed in his face. She rushed back to the stove. If she hurried, she would be done by the first commercial.

She poured oil on the pan. Because it seemed too much, she climbed up onto the counter once more for a paper towel, and, careful to place her finger tips in the thickest part of the crumple, soaked up the excess.

She dropped the towel and took her batter to the kitchen table so she could see the t.v. through the kitchen doorway. Agent Smart was gabbing into his shoe, then looking quizzical. "Chief?" "Chief?" Desperate "Chiieef!" as the shoe emitted a dial tone. Arne's heh heh blended into the canned laughter.

Something made her look back to the stove. The grease-soaked paper towel had caught fire, a brilliant orange and blue that jumped higher than she would have thought possible; it seemed to be grasping for the wooden cupboards above the stove.

A cry of 'Arne Arne' echoed in her mind but her voice was gone. She rushed silently over to the stove thinking salt? Baking soda? She couldn't remember exactly what you were supposed to put on a grease fire. She didn't think she could climb onto the counter next to the flame.

Her eyes swept over the sink, half full of soapy water. She grabbed a wet dish rag that floated on top of the dishes, and, shutting her eyes, whacked at the burning towel and frying pan, splashing suds and blown back bits of charred paper towel into the air.

The place where the dishrag hit the pan yowled like a scorched cat. Glowing embers bubbled in the air, and black bits too–like wisps of the scorched cat. Luckily, they all seemed to aim themselves towards the sink, and after rewetting the dishcloth, she merely smothered what was left of the burning paper towel, didn't bother with whacking any more.

"What the hell's going on in here?" Arne said, stomping into the kitchen.

"Goddammit," he said.

She was ready to hug him. She was ready to tell him everything. Tell him again.

"What are you trying to do now, idiot? Burn the whole goddamn house down?" He switched off the last burner. The frying pan, black blue inside, was smoking madly. "Jesus Christ." He grabbed a couple of potholders and, elbowing her out of the way, picked up the hot pan and sizzled it into the sink.

"God damn it, Les. Shit. Talk about stupid. Don't you understand anything?"

"Leave me alone," she said. She turned away from him. She shifted her body as he moved between the sink and stove to keep away.

"Christ Les, what's wrong with you anyway?" Arne said, "Jesus Christ."

'Christ Les, what's wrong with you anyway?' Now there was something— 'Christ Les, what's wrong with you anyway'–

So then, he didn't know. He hadn't understood a single stupid thing.

She turned to him in sudden relief–

"Look, I put it out," she said. "Calm down."

* * *

She lay straight and flat in her bed. A hint of smoke still hung about the house. Every time she breathed, it told her that she had to do something.

She wanted to go into Arne's room and plead with him, but that didn't make any sense anymore. It seemed that she hadn't told him after all, or if she had, he hadn't believed her.

So everything should be already okay.

She got up and got her notebook. She shut her door and turned on a very small lamp. She turned to a blank page. It was very white in the dim light. She picked up her pen.

"Dear Somebody," she wrote.

"How are you? I am fine."

Why did she always write that? You didn't have to write that. It wasn't a law.

She was tempted to cross it out, but didn't want to mess up the paper.

"Something has happened to me," she wrote. "Something bad. I can't tell anyone. But someday I will meet you and I will tell. I promise. Maybe you even know now. Maybe you will get this letter and know now. Please know now.

"Love, Les."

She tried not to read the note, tilting her eyes away as she ripped the page from her notebook, then folded it several times until it was a small wadded rectangle with frayed bits of spiral notebook fringing one side. Holding the wad in her fist, she stepped from her bed and tiptoed into the hallway.

She could hear her dad's snores through the door that shut in her parents' air conditioning, but she could see through the crack at the bottom that their light was still on. Arne's door, opposite, was also shut, but seemed dark. She tiptoed down the hall.

She stepped quietly down the basement stairs, squashing the fear that rose up in the stairwell. She turned on the light, she couldn't go down there in darkness, but forced herself to move slowly in order to be as quiet as possible, holding her one fist clasped, the other on the pine railing, listening with that palm to the small, almost indecipherable knots in the wood, as if they were some company.

She tried not to be sad. She tried to tell herself that maybe the person would get the letter right now. That maybe the minute she put it in its mailing place, someone would feel it.

The idea seemed to strengthen each tendon, push her feet along. But as she turned the corner into the actual basement, she had a sudden picture of Duke coming back. Parking his car in the same silent way he had unparked it, creeping in quietly, scratching his belly by the side of the downstairs bed like her father sometimes did, lying down, waiting.

Fear inhaled her. She made herself keep on. The floor tiles were brown with little bits of black. The shelves were sloppy with books. Certain titles jumped off the spines, their print bigger or darker or lighter than others. "The Valley of the Dolls." "Seven Days to Success." "Eat Fat and Grow Thin."

Eat fat and grow thin? She could sense her father behind that title, her father buying that book, and could breath again.

Finally, she got to the cupboard. Tucking the note under one arm, she worked quietly at the metal bolt that kept it closed. It came free with a small jab into her palm. The door swung open.

She was immediately hit by a smell of must and fabric. The uniforms so still. Creased ghosts in a dormitory. She pushed them along the rod.

She didn't want a winter one. Their wool itchy, their dark olive color like a grave. She could not possibly reach a person who would help in a uniform like that.

The summer ones were better, the light khaki gentler, almost welcoming, the cotton silken with wear and press. As she touched them she could imagine her dad as a young man (still with hair) smiling into a camera, his old dog Rustler by his knee, his science books ready to be packed, to be lugged along with him wherever.

The pants were thicker, sturdier, and there seemed to be several of them. But a shirt was what she wanted. She pulled the hangers quietly across the rod until she found one. It had little colored squares pinned to the left breast and there was a buttoned pocket with an insignia on it. Without taking the shirt from the hanger, without even unbuttoning the pocket, she slipped in her fold of letter, there, right below those little colored squares.

She flattened the pocket over the slight bulge of her note, smoothed it, and deliberately trying not to remember which shirt it was, swooped the other uniforms back along the rod to obscure it.

She tried to stop trembling, closed the cupboard, went back upstairs. The smell of smoke from the kitchen hit her like a wall. She breathed through her mouth. She could see from the hall that her parents' light was out now, the crack below their door darkly silent.

She slipped into her own bed slowly, her room so hot after the basement, so hot after everything. She got up again and went to open her parents' door with the thought that some of their air-conditioning might seep across the hall to her. When she lay down again, she thought she could almost feel it.

Arne
Suburban Maryland
August 1968

His parents were taking forever as usual. He could hear them in their bedroom, just next door.

His mother accused, "I never have time to read books."

His father whined, "I don't either."

"Yes, you do. Look at those paperbacks–there's a whole shelf full right there. And you've read them all, haven't you? Haven't you?"

He closed the door to his own room. Les had already gone out to wait in the car the way they always used to. Great, let her suffocate. He was going to stay in with the air conditioning.

Drawers were yanked open.

"Look at this," his mom complained. "All these drawers jammed up. It's no wonder I don't have any space for anything—'Save. Save. Save.' You've written 'Save' on one, two, three, four copies of this church program. I mean honestly, do we need four copies of this? And what about this one?"

Papers flapped onto the carpet.

"'Save,'" she said. "You've written 'save' on one, two, three, copies of that ad. Can you tell me why we need to save three copies of an ad?"

"Because it's important," his dad snarled.

Arne opened his bedroom door. "God damn it," he yelled into the hallway. "Are we going to go or not?"

The house was instantly quiet.

He shut his door again and walked back to his bed, feeling strong, his limbs long and loping. He wished his room were bigger, way bigger, so that he could walk and walk this private loping gait.

He thought of a picture his French teacher had put up on the bulletin board–roads in France–yellow dirt and skinny sparrow-twigged trees lining both sides. No people.

He thought of vistas out West. Endless sky, desolate plateau, not a car in sight.

He wished he had a road like that in here.

His father whined, "God damn it, Ing–let's just go, huh? Let's not go into all this stuff right now."

At his grandma's, there were dirt roads and there weren't many people, endless corn. But he'd never walked very far. They were roads leading to nothing.

Maybe it was the same in France. Out West. But he couldn't quite believe that. Things had to be different somewhere.

"Come on, Momma," his dad coaxed. "I'm just gonna pack the trunk now, okay?"

He kneeled on his bed to look through the blinds that clumped above his air conditioner. He pressed his nose to the glass. The bush by the outside wall was high so that he could only see the car through blurs of leaves.

Her profile came into view a moment, then disappeared again. He imagined her plumping up a pillow, one of the ones they took for the ride, turning it over to find a cool spot.

They used to both do that. Sit out hours before a trip, arguing about who would get which pillow, which side of the back seat, then where the dividing line was.

He sat down on the bed hard, mattress banging into the wall with his weight.

Why did he have to go anyway?

When he got up again, his legs felt brittle, his stomach an egg. He opened the door slowly, holding the twist tight to keep the knob from clanking.

His parents had moved from their bedroom. He peered towards the living room, but his parents didn't seem to be there either.

From his parents' bedroom window he could see them out by the car, his mom 's face cross and concentrated, all its lines focusing into a dark V which met at the tip of her nose. She directed it towards the trunk of the car, rearranging every bag his dad had put in.

He dialed quickly, wincing at the corrosive rattle of each dial.

"Lowell Residence."

"Hey Jas," he whispered.

"Arne? Is that you? Hey I thought you guys were gone–"

"You know my folks."

"Oh yeah."

"Listen Jasper," he paused. "You think I could stay with you?"

"What do you mean?"

"You know, today. This week. Well, I think it's closer to ten days. If I don't go with my parents?"

"Not go with your parents?"

"Yeah, you know. There's no way in hell they'll let me stay here by myself."

"No."

"I mean I could probably manage it–"

"Gee I don't know Arne," Jasper said doubtfully. "That's a long time all alone. No car–"

"Shit, Jasper, that doesn't matter. The point is could I stay with you guys?"

"Sure, I mean I guess I should ask my folks, but man, I think so–you know–I mean if you want to–"

"I want to."

"You want me to ask right now?"

"Let me talk to mine first. I'll say you invited me to something, I don't know, a special fishing trip."

"Sure, I guess so."

"Anything. It doesn't matter."

"But what if they ask my folks?"

"Shit Jas, they won't ask. I mean, we might go up to Shadyside anyway, right? And if we do, we might fish. But you should tell your folks I *have* to stay. Like I really need a place–"

Arne could hear the vibration of his dad's footsteps in the living room, gathering up another suitcase, outside door creaking, shuffle of bags hitting the door frame.

"Look Jas, I'll call you back."

"Sure Arne, have a good trip."

"Come on asshole, I'm not going on the trip."

"Oh yeah, okay, okay, I'll talk to my folks."

"Yeah, thanks."

From the bedroom window he could see his dad coming up the sidewalk banging inside.

It was stupid to talk to his dad first. It would be his mom 's deciding.

"Hey Dad–"

"You don't want to go?" his dad scowled, after Arne explained what he wanted.

"Look Dad, I've done it every single summer."

His father listened, shrugged. Then, frustration suddenly taking hold, he clenched his fists at his sides. "Not now," his voice sliding from despair to aggression and then back again. "Look, go talk to Momma. You don't want to go, then talk to her."

His mother was in the front seat of the car, arranging stuff by her feet and taking out the gum she only chewed on car trips and when she had to type something. It helped her concentrate.

Arne went to stand by her window.

In her seat at last, she seemed at perfect ease, all the arguments of the house forgotten. It was like they were already on the road. She opened up last Sunday's news magazine, the top magazine of a small stack on her lap, and began leafing through.

His stomach hit the window level, really his pelvis, cock in her face, he thought and leaned down quickly. Which was a mistake. It was instantly harder to talk like that, face to face too close in the open square of window, face to profile.

She didn't seem to notice him, looking through her magazine, chewing her gum, concentrating. Biting his lip, he watched her jaw work, eyes flicker. Her skin seemed poreless, impermeable, except at the nose, there he could just make out tiny openings along the bone.

His dad was behind him, coming down the sidewalk, his shirt ruffled, face red. Must have finished his last, last check. Yes, the iron downstairs was turned off.

"Mom," Arne said.

She read her magazine.

"Mom."

As she turned to him, the ridge of her nose, forehead glinted, reflecting the sun, the glossy magazine, iridescent paint of car. She put her hand on her forehead, her eyes seeming to rebel against her own shine. When she screwed her face up, she looked older, future wrinkles pressed into place, and birdlike, her straight nose the beak, her eyes dark and piercing.

('I'm sorry,' Les had cried.)

(What the hell?)

"I'm sorry Mom, but you know I really don't want to go this time," he said. "I just don't."

The slight question in his mother's eyes changed to complete bewilderment. It was as if he were speaking a different language.

"To Minnesota," he explained. "I just don't want to go."

"You don't want to go? What are you talking about?"

His dad lumbered by him, willfully not listening as he reopened the trunk, picked up the towel that protected the raincoats, then the raincoats, then poked among the suitcases.

"God damn it," he muttered.

"I'm not going," Arne said.

His dad cried out from the back of the car, "oh come on Arne, we're all ready now, let's just get going."

"Ssshh, Andrew. God, do you want the whole neighborhood to hear you?" Ingrid said. Then to Arne, "you can't stay here by yourself Arne, how can you stay here by yourself?"

"I'm not planning to stay here by myself."

He looked down to his sneakers. Why couldn't they just go, drive off? Why couldn't they openly forget about him?

"The Lowells said–the Lowells invited me to stay with them."

Arne could feel his mother scrutinizing his face, wandering over the bumps, the blackheads, the incipient eruptions. He looked away. Light green bushes at the corner–the ones his dad always complained would cause an accident and get them sued, dark brown telephone pole–street sign–Nathan Hill–the stretched-out row of houses lined up so straight you could only see their edges.

Third house down was different though. It was L-shaped, back farther than the others, at the end of a long blacktop driveway, treeless yard. The brick was darker than the others, not so red. The woman there had supposedly hung herself, the mother, he didn't remember ever seeing her, but he knew the kids–Lydia and Calvin, strange palefaced kids with fishly large lips, Jehovah's witnesses who never came out to play on the street, didn't get to go to the parties in school either, had to go down and sit in the principal's office Halloween, even Christmas. He could picture Lydia leaving the classroom, she was the one his age, so slow and white and grey-lipped she seemed to be bloodless.

She couldn't even have a cupcake. Shit.

"Look," he said, turning back to his mother. "I've always gone. Every single summer. I just don't want to this time."

Ingrid sighed. "Oh, come off it, Arne. You know perfectly well we're not going to leave you."

He wondered, staring at that house, who had found her. The father was a pale man, tall. He wore very black pants with the belt a little over the waist. There was something weird about that belt, too brown against the black, too thick, too much lip hanging the wrong side of the buckle, something weird.

Would be him, he supposed, the mother would plan that much. To greet the husband from her rope, maybe she even used a belt.

"Arne, we're all packed," his mother said. "There's lots of times you can stay at the Lowell's, but not now, not when we're about to take a trip."

"You can stay when we get back," his dad said.

"The point isn't to stay at the Lowell's," Arne said.

"Arne, it's all set," Ingrid said, eyebrows gathering into a point. "I'm not going to take stuff out of the suitcases. Besides, your grand-ma's expecting you. What do you have against your grandma?"

Arne looked back up the street. Fucking house.

"Has she ever done anything but be nice to you?

"It's not her," he said.

"Andrew, can you turn on the air conditioner? I'm not going to sit out in this hot car."

His dad started the motor quickly, pushing at several buttons at once.

"I don't need those clothes," Arne said.

"Arne." Ingrid's face grew white, eyes narrowed, nose seeming to lengthen. "I'm not going to leave you here to go to the Lowell's, I'm just not." She rolled up the window as she spoke, till it was only open a crack. "Andrew, would you just get him."

His father struggled out of the packed car.

"Look," he said, bending down to Arne, speaking quietly. "I know Momma's hard; this trip isn't all that fun for you, but we'll do some-thing special, I promise–I don't know what it will be, but something. You and Les, or just you, if you want."

'Andrew, just get him.' What the hell was she thinking? 'Just get him.' His dad wasn't one of the big belts.

"We don't have to do something special," Arne said.

"I know you'd rather spend time with Jasper," his dad said, putting out a hand to help him up. "At your age, you want to do your own things. Naturally."

There were kids he knew that could manage all of this, Arne thought, as he let his Dad take his hand. Wouldn't let themselves get trapped. Johnny Lowell for one. Always smooth-skinned, tan, cool. He would just not have gone, not once he set his mind to it.

Lydia, Calvin, those two could manage it too in their own way, could drive all the way to fucking California with you, not minding a fucking thing.

He got into the car on his father's side. Les scooted over quickly so their bodies didn't touch. He didn't look at her.

"Really, there are just things you have to do sometimes, Arne," his mother said, "even if they're not exactly what you want."

They drove forever. His mother read the paper, snapped her gum, said, "oh that damn McCarthy," and offered, every once in a while, to drive. His dad yawned, rubbed his eyes, said he was okay for now. All the time Les sat there quietly, looking out the window. It made him want to smash her face in.

He kept thinking of how Duke had taught him to hit a ball. It was not the kind of thing his dad could teach, could even do. But Duke could teach somebody to do anything physical, anything that had to do with sports.

He could remember the feel of his body next to his, the warp of his ribs through his flesh, cotton shirt, the weight of his muscles too, the breadth of arm, chest, shoulder. How light the bat was next to that, the mass of Duke.

It used to bother him that his dad was so different from most men in their neighborhood. Duke was different too, jovial, joking. The neighborhood men more grim, stodgy, straight. He hadn't exactly wanted Duke as a dad. His dad was smart, brilliant, sweet. He knew that Duke was not. Still, he had loved his easy gruffness, the way he cajoled people, the way he could turn just about anything into a game, a game he always seemed to win, or if not, a game he could have won, had he wanted to. That was how he made you feel anyway. And even got you to laugh about it.

He looked out the window. Stupid fucking country, flat as flat.

No wonder they wanted the stupid war, crackers. No wonder they couldn't understand a stupid thing but black and white. Not even that.

There weren't even real farms near the turnpike, just flat land, every once in a while a brace of trees, a fence. Houses hiding.

His sister sitting there.

He wanted to tell her to just shut up. But she was quiet.

The silence was almost worse than talking, so incessant, so heavily there. The slow water torture of silent nothing talk.

The drip drop drip of blame.
So what so what so what.
Car clacked, gum snapped.
Drip drip drip drop drop.

* * *

He tried to think about a math problem like the kind his dad used to make up when they were waiting for food in a restaurant: 'if one train goes in one direction 100 miles per hour and another goes in another direction 60 miles an hour and they go one hour—'

He wanted it to take up his whole brain.

'And the directions they go are at an angle of 90 degrees.'

'No, make that 45 degrees.'

Yes or no yes or no. Drip drip drip drop drop.

Something must have happened, he was sure of that much–

Fuck, he felt his own dick hardening.

Go away.

It wasn't that, it had nothing to do with that, she'd tell Mom about that.

Les had opened the window and lay her head on the frame so that air blew right into her face. It whipped over onto his side too. There was a ton of air at seventy miles an hour, air and zoom.

Her face looked so small like that, her eyes Chinese, wind blowing her hair back like someone pulling it into a knot.

Her face seemed to deny the force of wind. She held it as if she were asleep.

It made him furious.

Wake up goddamn it.

He leaned over and rolled up her window.

"Arne!" she cried.

"I can't even think it's so loud."

She reached for the handle, but he stuck his elbow over her to keep her in place.

'Mo-om,' he heard next in his mind. 'Mo-om, Arne's hurting me,' he imagined, able to compose the tones without missing a beat. 'I'm not hurting her,' he'd say, 'I'm not even touching her.'

But she was silent. She did not say, 'Mo-om'.

He sat back in his seat. He stretched out his legs on the floor across the hump in the middle, straight onto her side of the car, but he did not look at her, he looked out. Babump babump. A silence of land out there, the same flat nothing.

Why wouldn't she say, 'Mo-om'? 'Mo-om stop him'?

She was supposed to say 'Mom' now.

He crossed his arms over his chest. There was a fence along this part of the highway, with brown slats, rooftops just behind. Who could live like that, beside a stupid highway, in a stupid plastic house, whizz all day long, whizz, whizz.

He tried to go back to the problem of the trains. Forty-five degrees. They used to have trains out here. He'd ridden one once he knew, though he barely remembered it. He supposedly had a big fight with his mom about having to wear a grey suit coat and short pants. He didn't fight about the suit coat, it was the short pants. She'd told him about it enough times, how he'd wanted long pants.

What he remembered was standing by the conductor when they got on, the open door of the train, the steps up from the platform, smoke pouring out in all directions. It must have been smoke mixed with fog, there seemed so much of it, as if the engine were taking over the sky.

Babump babump, even with the window shut, you could hear the tires. His mom was asleep now, head back, no gum. His dad didn't care much for the radio.

"Hey look," he mumbled to his sister as he bent over to her door again, to roll down the window. "You want the window open."

He lay down. Les had gone to sit up next to their mom because she felt sick. He could hear them talking and he imagined them, Les holding their mom's hand, their mom with her arm about her.

"How big is your ring?" Les asked, must be fingering it. "I mean in carats."

"It's 3/4 of a carat," Ingrid sighed. He imagined her holding her hand out straight to display it better, examine it too. "It's a good stone, but Daddy should have probably gotten one, one carat exactly. There's really no point in less than one. It's just not as valuable." His father groaned beside them.

"Oh Andrew," she went on. "Though this is an awfully nice one, really it is."

"Can I try it on?" Les asked.

"No, sweetie, not in the car. I don't want to take it off in the car."

One carat, one carat. Can I try it on?

Why doesn't she fucking say to her, 'look, I'm in trouble, mom. I've gone insane.'

He felt a sudden wave of nausea.

He wished he had a little box he could put his head into. A little box that would know everything, wouldn't even have to bother, knowing so much.

Knowing nothing–all the nothing he knew–hit him like a sea rolling beneath his feet and then on top of him, stupid to lie down in the back after eating all that shit at the rest stop–

He sat up as if his torso were a container he might spill; he held onto the door handle.

"Please mom, I won't lose it," she said.

"I think I should just wear it for now," her mom said, "in a moving car and all."

Beads of sweat formed on his forehead, his stomach swerved. He tried alternately to concentrate on and ignore the simple fact that he hated the whole goddamn lot of them.

It seemed forever. It was forever. Through the cornfields and the no-fields and the gas stations and the Stuckey signs, and then as the sky darkened, the occasional smell of skunk.

A forever of sadness held him beneath the darkening sky.

What he doubted: that anyone–a girl–would just take him, put his head upon her lap (he thought of an ad for a Swedish movie–the man pretending to rest, his hair stroked back, his head cradled, loved, it seemed, just for laying there like a log.)

His skin hurt. The turquoise upholstery scraped the backs of his arms like fish scales; maybe he was allergic to something, his chest a too-tight balloon.

He looked at Les who looked out the window. The forever flat wings of the turnpike.

In France, there were poppies along the roadsides. He'd seen pictures of them, a kid in his class who'd gone to France and posed, one in her hair–

Les would be like that, he thought. No matter what happened, she'd put this big red poppy in her hair, smile for the camera.

No, it was really his mother who'd be like that, his mother *with* Les, gathering poppies for her hair, sticking one behind Les' ear, just so, repeatedly.

He imagined himself pitching out of the car, bopping around between tires with his hands up over his face as they stood there, practicing their poses.

He smiled.

They drove into the night. He and Les were quiet in the back. Her mom had given up on gum, even on the newspaper, too dark to read now. She half-slept shaking herself into consciousness every once in a while to say urgently, "you okay, Andrew?!"

The headlights of other cars peered through the windshield. They felt to him like searchlights, he thought of Vietnam, guys there, going there, the fear of a light in the dark, the fear of no light. He sank lower in his seat, his feet against the seat back in front, low.

They stopped at a motel. His dad said he just couldn't go anymore. They were lucky to get a vacancy this late as it was.

They stayed in one room with two double beds. He lay in the big double bed next to his father. His dad fell asleep very quickly, his paperback next to his face, even forgetting to take his glasses off. Les and his mom were in the other bed just across, sleeping too.

It felt like the kind of room people were supposed to meet in Playboy cartoons–the woman's breasts hanging out, the guy screwing in his socks, the angry husband bursting in, some joke about–oh yes—'I thought he just meant washing the windshields when he said full service'.

Mustard color rugs, mouthwash blue bathroom.

His chest hurt. Motels chock full of molds, old rugs, a piece of shit. He rubbed his nose. He turned over to his side. He imagined himself suddenly walking hand in hand with a faceless girl, tall enough, long-haired, in the caverns of the new shopping mall that just went up near them. He didn't care about big boobs, screwing around, someone to talk to, someone tall enough, long-haired.

* * *

Finally, Wisconsin. There were rocks. Gray rocks gnarled like tree trunks. Tall cliffs of rocks. Tree trunks of rocks. After the flatness of Indiana and Illinois, it was like a drink of cool water.

He tapped his leg, trying to keep his hand from forming a fist.

"How much longer?" he said, leaning up towards his dad.

"Oh we're not so far now. Isn't this the place where we saw the Indian Mounds?" his mom said. "Sure it is. Remember! We took a day-trip down from Grandma's."

"Oh yeah," Arne said. "They had that stupid movie and then we walked through the park."

"And they had that great cheese," his dad grinned. "Fresh from Wisconsin."

Arne groaned.

"Yes, that's right," Ingrid said, slowly as if she were looking back over her brain. "They had that huge cheese store. We went there that time too, right?"

"Yes, it's not far from here either," his dad said, "about half-an-hour. You want to stop?"

"I didn't mean we should stop there now," Ingrid said. "I just wanted to see if I remembered right."

""We could just stop at the store for a few minutes," his dad said. "It's about… let's see…."

The car swerved as he calculated.

"Eleven miles from here. Well, better make that twelve—But that's there and back—."

"Oh Andrew, let's not do it now," Ingrid said. "Do we really need to do it now?"

"Awww," he scowled. "We never stop when it's something I want to do."

"What <u>time</u> is it?" Arne snarled.

"What? Oh…around two."

"Their time?"

"Their time, yes."

"It was awfully good cheese, real Wisconsin cheese," his dad moaned.

"Andrew, they have cheese all over Wisconsin," his mom said.

"So you want to stop?"

He remembered the Indian mounds as humps of grass. Duke had come down on the trip with them and, acting the fool like always, kept asking how the Indians had known about camels.

They drove over a long bridge made of iron crosses. The Mississippi.

"So you don't even want to stop for a minute?" his dad moaned, his face contorted with disappointment.

"Do you really want to? Now when we're almost home?"

"Christ woman, how many times do we get a chance to have real Wisconsin cheese?"

"Every single day at the grocery store," Arne muttered.

"Hush Arne. Oh Andrew, you really want to stop?" his mom said.

"Yes, *I Do*." His dad's voice was like a child's. His lower lip stuck out.

He hated it when his dad got like this. He couldn't even feel sorry for him.

"Okay, okay, stop then," Ingrid said. "You're the one that has to do the driving, I guess. If you want to stop, then stop."

"Christ," Arne growled, but his dad's face lightened immediately and he sped up the car.

"Anyway, we can get some for Grandma," he said. "She likes cheese."

"That's right," Ingrid said. "We can get some for Grandma."

Arne shook his head. "Jesus."

"Well, Grandma probably *would* like some cheese," Les said.

The place was called "The Mound of Cheese" in black letters on a big white sign, the kind that usually referred to things like 'Pizza Night--Tues.' and 'Happy Birthday Stan'.

Arne didn't want to get out of the car. No, that wasn't right. He was desperate to get out of the car, but he wanted to make a point of not getting out, he wanted to make his parents feel guilty. Except that they didn't seem to notice when he had stayed in the car, they trooped off into the store; they just went ahead of him.

Shit.

It was a white place with low ceilings, fluorescent lights, the waxy bars stacked up like gold in Fort Knox, the spreads in bright little containers.

His dad wasn't picky. As long as they got something.

But his mom wanted to pick and choose carefully now they were there. She wasn't going to get just anything.

And now Arne felt incredibly hungry. His mom always watched everything so carefully on trips. Not wanting to waste food or money. Not seeming to think calories were necessary for just sitting in the car.

They had samples, thank God. Little scrapes of spread on crackers. The spreads looked dubious: one had big bits of red and green mixed in, one was speckled with some kind of brown spice. Even the plain one was suspiciously orange, and peaked with an odd squiggle. But he was starved.

He took one sample in his right hand, and then shifted it into his left, where he cupped it by his side, so he could take another.

Just then, his dad walked up.

"Look, what they have here," he said loudly, trying to make a point about how great everything was.

His dad ate the cheese crackers eagerly–one, two, three. "You get one, Arne?"

"Dad—" he said.

"Here."

"No, I got some."

His dad smiled broadly, teeth shiny with glee and, Arne suspected, cheese. "It's good, huh? Real Wisconsin cheese. Fresh."

"It's okay."

His mom stepped up to the counter, carrying a couple of waxen blocks.

"You think Sharp's too strong," she asked Les. "I know Daddy likes it, but I think it might be a little strong."

"Ing, Ing, did you see this?" his dad beamed. "Free samples!" He picked one up and rushed across the store to give it to her.

"Oh Andrew," his mom groaned, but she took the sample all right.

"Pretty good, huh?"

Ingrid shut her eyes, shivered. "You like that mixed-up stuff, don't you? Well, look, how about these?"

Listening to his parents talk about what cheese they should get, watching Les listen to them, the smooth curve of her profile unperturbed, he felt furious again.

He went over to her. His walk felt the exact opposite of the long loping walk of the morning before. It was a squinched, shuffling walk, cramped from the hours in the car, flattened by the endless nothing, and too, by his sister's silence.

He pulled her sleeve.

"Stop it," she whispered.

"I don't want you to sneak around and eat it all," his mom said.

"I won't," his dad sighed.

Arne pulled Les by the sleeve towards the doorway, then awkwardly, out of the door.

"Arne," she hissed. "Stop it."

He kept a tight hold. He had her now, he thought.

"What do you want?" she said.

"Leave me alone," she whispered.

His parents came out and they followed them back to the car. Now he wished he had just stayed in it after all, it was so awful getting back in, like squeezing into a little gelatin capsule, spaceship, the air as stale as a locker.

"Okay, maybe I shouldn't say anything. But you'd blow up like a balloon if I didn't. You know you would," his mom said up front.

"I wouldn't," his dad said.

Arne leaned his head against the window, shut his eyes, trying to keep in mind the fact that they were almost there, and that after being there a while, they'd leave.

Les
Dime, Minnesota
August 1968

Minnesota had seemed like a dream when she was littler, the place where summer let her hair down. Every day the sky was blue to the ground, the grass green out to the horizon, the air just warm enough in the sun, just cool enough in the shade. Her grandmother was the kind of person who loved completely, loved in a quiet, comfortable way that only asked the other person to sit there and eat once in a while.

Normally, there were a couple of cousins. Others visiting at the same time.

And sometimes there was Duke. He too liked Minnesota in summer, liked visiting their grandmother, though she wasn't his grandmother, his mother, that is. He would be silly with them and then take them places too, go-cart riding and miniature golf, maybe even real golf, or out to the farm to pick apples.

But this time, there was nobody. Chickens her grandma had gotten that strutted around a shed on the far side of the lawn, were fun for a few minutes. Arne would have played with her with a cousin, but without one, he was good for nothing but mean stares over the books he read. Her dad was taking advantage of the time to lie down and read too ('that sure was an awful long drive,' he kept saying). And her mom was working. This was what she always did when they went to

Grandma's. Put on old clothes, pinned her hair back, stood around with one hip out like a disgruntled teenager, and then scraped, spackled, painted, put down new tile, went shopping for a rug or pillows or bedspread. "Just," as she said, "fixed things up a little."

Her grandma sat at the kitchen table, wishing, as she always did, that Ingrid would stop.

"I like people to have a good time when they visit me," she said, fingering the oilcloth. "Not work all the time."

Ingrid, who was painting the kitchen cupboards, stopped a minute to look at what she'd just covered.

"I sure wish you wouldn't work so hard," Grandma sighed.

"Oh Mom, come on. I like doing this. It's fun fixing up someone else's house—not like doing your own," Ingrid chuckled, wiping her head with the back of her hand. "It's always that way."

"Oh, so you wouldn't touch your own but you like mucking around in mine," Grandma said.

"Besides, you're allowed to have things nice aren't you? To have things nice once in a while?"

"Come on Ing. Those old cupboards were good enough. They opened and shut, didn't they?" She sighed. "I just hate to have you work all the time."

"You might as well just let her, Grandma," Les said. "She's not going to stop."

"She could at least let us help her. Don't you like painting, sister?" she gave Les a surprisingly hard pat on her upper arm. "You look like you got a pretty strong arm there."

"She won't let us help her either," Les said. "She doesn't think we can do it right."

"Stop it Les," Ingrid said. "It's not that. It's just, well, I've got it going now." She leaned back a moment to look, dabbed one corner. "I've got the hang of this old paint. You know it takes a certain touch, this paint. Oh, darn it all, why does it drip like that?" She took a rag and wiped the counter. "This wood's got a funny surface too."

"Those old cupboards never were any good," Grandma said. "And I don't know why you didn't get fresh paint. I've got money, you know, money for paint."

"Oh Mom, I thought I might just use it up. And once it's on, it looks nice enough. If you do it careful." She studied the shiny cream enamel.

"See, I told you she wouldn't let us," Les said.

"Oh, come on. Can't you just let me get on with it?" Ingrid said. "Oh darn it," giving another swipe at the counter.

Les looked down, throat hurting.

"Hey!" Grandma said, giving Les another slap on the arm. "How about we do some baking, huh? Those two old boys in there going to be hungry before long, even with that paint smell griping their bellies. Too late to bake bread, but I wouldn't say no to a nice cake. How about you, Miss?"

She leaned over her shoulder. "That's not going to bother your painting now, is it Ing? If we bake a cake?"

Ingrid frowned. "It might be better to do it another time, don't you think? I don't want things to get all sticky."

"Oh, Ing."

"Okay, okay. But just keep it over there, huh? And watch out you don't get paint in the batter."

Grandma raised her eyebrows towards Les. "As if we didn't know any better than that," she whispered.

* * *

Les didn't know why Grandma called the tablecloth an oilcloth. It looked just like ordinary plastic to her. Maybe it had to do with the soft felt that coated one side. Or maybe it had something to do with the way water beaded up on it when you wiped it up, sort of like oil.

Her mother was doing that now, wiping. She had finished the cupboards. Les was frosting the angel food cake she and her grandmother had made.

The color of the frosting hadn't turned out quite right. She'd wanted lilac and it ended up bruise.

"I think it's pretty," her grandma said. "Looks real nice, that deep purple."

"It's certainly original," Ingrid said.

It hurt her that it wasn't right, that it was one more thing she'd messed up. Maybe her mom was right about the cupboards.

She'd wanted it to be special, a cake like her grandmother, white like her hair, lilac like her favorite dresses. She was especially glad now that Duke wasn't there, thinking how he'd laugh at her.

Her arm trembling slightly, she reached over the cake to spread the purple onto the far side. It brushed against the skin at the base of her forearm as if it really were a bruise.

"You know sister," her grandmother said. "You can just swivel that plate around a bit, like this," she reached over, wrinkled fingers tipped with yellowing nails. "Then you don't have to reach so far."

* * *

She lay in the grass beside the apple tree. She had placed herself so that her body was completely in the sun except for her head, which just intercepted the shade of tree and house.

It was an old tree, the same kind they had at home, with those soft yellow summer apples. But unlike their tree at home, it had been pruned enough when it was young that there was open space underneath.

She lay on the grass, without a blanket, sniffing the occasional whiff of apple and twitching at the occasional crawl of bugs. They were the type of bugs that she could never actually find when she sat up to brush them away. Bugs, she had learned, that you just had to try to ignore.

He was supposed to come any day. She'd heard her Grandma talking about it, her mom complaining.

When she thought of him, she felt a shiver through her limbs. She edged herself farther into the sun, not getting up but shifting her hips up and down as if she were an angular snake, getting the base of her face, her neck, her chest, fully in the heat.

She imagined herself, sitting on his lap in her grandmother's kitchen.

'I'm too big to sit on your lap,' she said inside.

'What do you mean you're too big?' he said, and suddenly he was fiddling with her bra straps. 'You got a bra? Oh Les. What do you need a bra for? Catch food falling down your shirt? Ah baby.'

She imagined him pressing his hands against her sides, his thumbs over her nipples.

She felt her cheeks get hot, red. She thought of the boys from the bus, Arne's bus, always yelling at each other. 'You piece of shit,' they yelled.

She pictured, on the grass at the school bus corner, a pile of blackish turds buzzing with flies, the boys yelling.

She felt a weight in the grass next to her and the chill of real shadow. She made her face as smooth as it would go. Opened her eyes.

It was Arne.

She shut her eyes again, trying to stop her cheeks burning.

"You want to take a walk?" he asked, kicking her foot lightly.

"Where to?" she said, trying to seem casual.

"Christ, I don't know. Where's there to go? Either into town or out of it."

"Into town," she said and got up quickly, the bugs below her legs stinging like crazy now. "You got any money?"

"What do you want?"

"I don't know—candy?"

"I've got enough for that."

They walked silently to town. He carried a baseball, which he passed back and forth between his hands.

Her silence was consciously sullen. Why had he wanted her to come if he wasn't going to say anything?

He rubbed his nose, his face crinkled against the sun. He tossed the ball from one hand to the other.

She listened to the slap of the ball hitting his hand.

When they got to the park, she ran away from him, pushing around the merry-go-round. It wasn't a real merry-go-round, simply a small turning circle of benches. Then onto the swings for a bit, then over to the water tower which she began to climb.

Arne kept his distance, but she could feel him watching. He seemed like an adult standing there. A stupid adult. Why couldn't he just be like a kid once in a while? A stupid kid.

She climbed the metal ladder of the water tower. She imagined, as she climbed, that each step higher took her that much farther from him, made her that much more of a kid. Not a stupid kid, a cool kid. The kind that climbed and laughed and was always skinny and didn't care about anything.

The ladder was cut into segments, going from heavy metal slats to thinner and thinner rails. As she climbed up, the railing at the sides of the ladder became fine inside her palms, and the grass seen through the steps looked neater and neater, like a park groomed by sheep instead of footprints.

"Les, come down," he shouted.

"Leave me alone," she shouted down.

"You're too high."

She could see him at the base of the tower, her little brother now, his face dark and twisted.

"I'm not so high," she called down. "Scaredy cat."

"Les, stop being an idiot."

She realized that in fact she was higher than she had ever been. She'd never actually gone higher than the place where the thick ladder connected to the narrower one. Now she was even up to the next narrower.

"*You're* being an idiot," he called again.

She was afraid, looking down. But the sight of him, the sound of him, filled her with determination. He was always so mean to her. When she always tried to be nice. And he'd been allowed to be mean. While she'd had to be nice, always, as if it were some rule, but a rule for girls only. She raised her foot up to the next step, then the next.

"Les," he shouted.

When she looked out to the other side, she could see the post office. She usually went there in the morning with her grandma, sometimes even by herself, to pick up the mail. They didn't deliver out to her grandmother's house.

She couldn't see the post office itself though, it was wedged back into the buildings, what she could see was the American flag. It looked like a big postage stamp down there, a postage stamp at an angle, the stamp put on with a shaky hand.

It made her think of the American flag at her school, all those days raising it. Though at a distance like that, the colors looked so much lighter than her school flag, like way she used to imagine flags to look before she'd worked with one.

And then she felt sick. The grass too green, the sky too blue, the flag too damn small, the metal hand rails smaller, too damn small and cold and grey.

"Come on Les," Arne shouted. "Please."

"Okay okay," she called, trying to keep cockiness in her voice.

She brought her feet back down, one then the other, then the next again.

"I could go higher, you know," she shouted down.

"You *could* be an idiot."

Low enough to feel safe, she began posturing, hanging off one side of the railing. He groaned, but it was a silly groan. She was so low now she could almost jump.

"Why do you always have to do those things? Always," he said when she clambered up from the grass.

"Just because you're a scaredy cat doesn't mean I have to be."

"Just because I'm not an idiot doesn't mean you have to be."

"Arne, stop it."

He squinted up into the sun. He tossed his ball up with one hand, caught it with two. Most of the park was thick with shade, but they'd managed to find a hot spot. "So you want to get a drink?"

"You got enough money?"

"Yeah."

They walked to a little grocery a couple of blocks from the park. Arne got a coke, Les a fireball.

They sat on the curb in front of the store, Arne needing to drink the coke there to return the bottle. Les sucked on her fireball.

"Boy, this is hot," she said, fanning her tongue.

Arne stared at her. "Your tongue is red, you know. I mean, bright red."

"I bet." She looked down at the smooth concrete of the step, his long fingers supporting himself. His skin had always been yellower than hers. She knew it was just the way he was, his genes, but it had always seemed like part of his being a boy, him yellow, her pink.

"Thanks for buying it for me."

He nodded, eyes squinting away from her.

Everything felt so easy on the stoop. As smooth as cement. Made in the shade. Fanning her mouth repeatedly, she acted out the part of the younger sister, a lot younger. He hardly ever let her play that anymore, telling her to stop being so stupid. But he seemed to just absorb it now, to just sit quietly next to her, drinking it all in.

"This sure is a slow town," she said.

He drained his bottle and sighed, but did not stand up. It seemed to her that he was unwilling to break up their sudden ease.

It made her want to help him stay still; he seemed the important one. She jumped up. "You want me to take in your bottle?"

"Nah. Oh sure, okay."

Dim in the store. Blinking. Old guy at the counter, shirt bunched into his pants. Would be out here.

She swang back into the daylight. But even though she'd let him stay still, everything had changed.

"Christ what a town," he said, bursting out from his seat to the street corner.

"I got your money, Arne," she tried, skipping after him with the deposit.

"Shit. Two cents? Forget about it."

"Well, I don't have a pocket." She held out the pennies.

"Christ, I'll take them then." He jammed the coins into his pants, then, after a moment, fished them out. Squinted at the dates. Sighed, jammed them in again.

They walked back, she still skipping determinedly.

His steps slowed as they drew back to their grandmother's.

"Hey, let's go on for a change. You know, up there." He gestured with his head towards the dirt road that took over the blacktop once the road passed their grandmother's yard.

"Okay."

He tossed his hard ball onto the lawn.

He walked more slowly on the dirt road, though his stride was still long enough to keep a little ahead of her. She let him stay ahead, liking to be a step or two behind. She always liked not having to look ahead when she walked, but especially on a road like this, so empty, its thin band disappearing like infinity, cornfields on both sides.

She didn't really like the corn. It didn't feel like abundance, only humidity. It seemed to make her ears buzz, her gaze catch the edge of her nose awkwardly. And that made her remember that she didn't want to talk to Arne, that he couldn't be trusted. She kept her eyes to the ruts; the orange raking of ridge and collapse.

He stopped. "So what are you going to do?"

"What do you mean do?"

"He's coming back tomorrow you know."

"Who?"

"Duh!"

"Who said?"

"You didn't hear them talking about it? Mom? Grandma? Oh maybe he'll be a couple of days late. Sure. It's possible. Except that he already is late. Didn't you hear them?"

"I don't know."

"Come on, Les."

Her face reddening, she turned and started walking away from him, back to their grandma's house. She tried to ward him off with her back.

But he ignored her back. His steps seemed to curve around hers, to hook her beside him.

"Look, Les," he said. "I'm sorry about—oh you know, getting so mad at you all the time."

She tried not to react, but felt her face tightening. She never was able to mask anything.

"It's just when you told me that....well, shit, I mean, you don't hear something like that everyday. I didn't know what to think about it. Didn't want to think about it."

"So, don't."

"Aw, come on Les. Look, I want us to be friends."

"What do you know about friends?"

"Like a real brother and sister. Okay, I guess real brothers and sisters fight, sure, but I don't want us to be like that. At least not all the time... We could be like...I don't know... like a brother and sister in a book," he smiled apologetically. "You know, a book where they get along."

"The only brothers and sisters I can think of from a book are the Bobbsey Twins, and Arne, you and I don't qualify."

"Shit. So not like in a book. And maybe we'll still fight. I can't actually imagine not fighting with you. God, the way you act sometimes, so stupid."

"Don't say stupid."

"But sometimes you *are* stupid; there's just no other word for it."

"You want to be friends and then you go and call me stupid?"

"Okay, look, I'm sorry. Look, can't we sit down or something. I can't talk with you acting like you're going to run off any minute."

"Sit here?" She pointed to the ditch on the side of the road.

"Not there. Look at those bugs. Jesus, they'll eat us alive. How about in the middle of the road. Right here?" he dragged his foot across the dirt. "Nobody comes down this road anyway."

"We come down it."

"We don't count."

She sat down cross-legged, but felt too exposed in the middle of the road and got up almost immediately. She stumped over to the side. It was better with tall grass at her back, weeds as high as herself, and behind them big corn. It was better even with the bugs. She felt a lightness squatting, her limbs a stretchy as rubber bands. Arne sighed, followed her, clumped down heavily.

"So, what do you want to talk about?" she said.

Arne squinted up at the sun, swiping in front of him with his hand.

"Huh?" she said.

Frowning, he picked up a rock and tossed it hard, overhand, into the corn field on the opposite side of the road.

"Arne."

"Shit, look, I just wanted to ask you... I mean I know the answer already so it doesn't really matter what you say, but, I don't know, I guess I just want to hear it again from you. If that was true, you know, that stuff you told me about Duke?"

"Look, I saw you smoking grass, you and Jasper," she said.

"Shit Les. You didn't see us smoking any grass."

"No," she stammered, "but I know you did it."

"God damn it, Les, so what? Yes, we smoked some grass. Big shit."

"It is big," she said, scrunching her neck into her shoulders.

"So, what are you going to do? Run off and tell Mom. Tell on me?" He picked up a handful of rocks and threw them across the road. A scatter of dust and pebbles fell like a curtain from the arc of the toss.

"Stop it." She covered her head with her hands.

He picked up another handful.

"Arne," she said.

He threw that bunch too, shattering the air in front of them. And then another. Where they sat was now all dust.

She hunkered down between her knees, breathing in the small gap below her legs. He coughed.

She waited till he was done, not done exactly, just till he coughed a little less. Then taking her hands off her head, she looked over to him.

"You know you really shouldn't smoke stuff like that, Arne," she said. "Someone like you shouldn't smoke anything."

"Jesus Christ, Les, will you get off it about the smoking? I've done it once, twice, I don't know. It's not like I'm dealing the stuff."

"You better not."

She got up slowly, dusting the back of her shorts with her hands. She felt immensely relieved, almost light again.

"You can't just get out of it like that, you know," he said.

"Like what?" She tried to act nonchalant. God, she hated her face. So easily red, read.

The air where she stood was above his fading dust cloud, but thick with the moist hot breath of the corn.

"Come on Les," Arne said.

Stupid stupid.

"Look, it's okay," he said.

"It is not okay," she said.

"Shit, I don't mean it like that. Look, I'm your brother."

"My torturer."

He stood. "I admit I haven't been so good."

She glared at him.

"So, I've been bad," he said. "But it's just been teasing, you know that—"

"Pulling my hair—hitting me—making fun of me—"

"When did I hit you? Look, I'm trying to help now. I mean, I was thinking, who do you have but me? Unless you *want* to talk to Mom."

"I could talk to Grandma."

"Grandma! Give her a heart attack?"

"There's Dad."

"Well, he'd tell Mom. Make a huge to-do."

"So, I could tell them both," she said. "Anyway, there's nothing to tell. Except on you."

She wiped her eyes with her fingers, rubbed damp cheeks against her wrist. She looked down the yellow dirt road towards the town. It was better in that direction, broken up by trees, houses.

"You know you really shouldn't smoke that stuff Arne," she said. "Not even once. You could get arrested and everything. Then what would you do?"

He started back towards the house. "You know what you can do," he said. "Just go to hell."

* * *

Duke came that afternoon with golf clubs in tow. He'd won a tournament. He'd bet on himself too, so he'd really cleaned up, he laughed.

He gave her grandma, her mom, her dad and even Arne who turned away big hugs. Not touching her.

He didn't mention the basement; he didn't mention why he'd left their house so suddenly. Ingrid didn't either. Not in the flush of first meeting.

Grandma didn't keep beer in the house, but he had some out in his car. He kept going out there and getting one, and gave one to her dad who laughed, "oh sure. A nice cold beer tastes good once in a while. Even when it's warm."

The sky was a pale lake blue that night, its coolness coloring the grass, the barns, the white house across the street, the picket fence at the end of the field, as if they were seen through water. The kitchen seemed so yellow in comparison, all but the bruise-colored cake, and the shiny cream cupboards. Les' face felt hot; she could smell herself when she moved her arms, even through the paint smell. She tried to stay still.

"Let me do that, Ing," Duke said to her mom, taking the serving dish full of hot string beans that she carried. Then, with the other hand, he made a big show of pulling out her mother's chair. After all that, he turned to her grandma and bowed.

"What's got into you?" Grandma said. "You're going to be like one of those Englishy guys now? What do they call 'em? A footman!"

"A footman. Yes!" He squatted down next to Grandma, picked up her foot, which was bound in anklet and oxford, put it on his knee. Then he began rubbing the dry skin of her shin.

"Hey!" she said, laughing and trying to pull her foot back. "Get off my dusty old shoe, you."

"I'm just trying to be your footman," he growled, reaching to the floor behind him to balance himself.

"Well, get up! Real footmen don't sprawl around on the floor, do they?"

"How do I know what real footman do?" he said, jumping up. "I'm just a poor boy from Minnesota."

He played the scene, all of his scenes, for everyone but her. She could not quite understand how he managed it. He was as jokey as ever, more jokey. As gruff, more gruff. As physical, more physical. The difference was that none of the jokes, the physicality, not even the gruffness included her. If he happened to look in her direction, his eyes were blank, did not register her shape. But she could tell, from an angle, that they were alive again the minute he looked away.

She didn't think that the others even noticed it, except perhaps Arne. But Arne also avoided her looks too, so she couldn't actually be sure.

She realized now that she had hoped that he loved her–Duke. Like Ashley and Scarlett, Romeo and Juliet, Rhett and Scarlett. That he'd loved her so much he just couldn't stop himself. That that was the reason for everything. But it seemed now that that was wrong; that, of course, it was wrong.

* * *

She had to pee. But the bathroom was right off the living room, right in the center of everything. People would know if she went there. She was going to have to go outside.

She tiptoed out to the front porch and then down the flaking grey steps. She walked in a stiff-armed way, trying to hold everything in. She walked stiffly past the water pump, past the clothesline, through the soft green Minnesota grass.

She had thought that she would go behind the old cowshed. No one would be able to see her there, not from the house anyway. But as she made her way towards the shed, she remembered that there was a lot of trash behind it, sharp stuff too, like old tin cans and bits of wire fencing, splintered boards with nails sticking through them.

So, that wouldn't be good.

She looked around the large flat yard. Her grandmother's house was at the very edge of town. The yard opened up into a large field on one side, and just across the roads that intersected at its corner were acres of corn. On the other side was her grandmother's garden. She stepped carefully onto its black earth, watching out for the rows of vegetables, and for the little plastic wind-wheels shaped like daisies, sneaking looks over her shoulder. Could they see her from here?

Her toes sank into the crumbly black loam between the vegetables. The cabbages were immense, the kale even bigger. They would be best. But as she tried to crouch behind the navy green leaves, she realized that even they weren't high enough. She could be seen easily through the kale, and if they saw her they'd probably be madder than ever. 'How could you pee in the garden?' they would say.

She stood up holding her knees together tightly. She started walking towards town. She could go behind the band shell in the park, she thought. The highway was visible from there but hardly any cars drove by.

But when she got a block or so from her grandmother's, a large dog stepped out on the sidewalk.

It was a grey dog, white markings. The white places reminded her of the white of an eye, that part that almost looks blue.

It was a big dog. It came right up to her, sniffing around her legs and bottom.

She stood very still. "Good boy," she whispered to the dog, "good boy." There were tears of fear in her voice, but she tried to cover them. "Good boy."

Actually, it didn't seem a bad dog. It didn't seem like it would bite her. Still, she couldn't possibly go to the bathroom with a big dog sniffing at her legs.

She turned back towards her grandmother's house, walking very slowly. Once home, she could shut the dog in a car, she kept thinking, then she would be okay.

But as she got back into her grandmother's yard, the dog seemed to have disappeared. So she didn't have to worry about a car. She just had to find a place to pee.

She decided on the place behind the shed after all. The chickens were all gone, that was good. She waded through the long weeds slowly, using her feet to fold the long leafy stalks over all the ends of fencing, protruding nails, over anything that looked man-made, using the leaves as a cushion.

Finally, she got squarely behind the shed. But when she bent to pull down her shorts, she realized that her legs were covered with blood. The stalks had been bristly with points, the leaves too, and everywhere they had touched, they had cut.

She woke up just in time, thank god. She got up quickly, awkwardly. It was crowded by her cot, and so cold. She wished she didn't have to pee too cold to get up how could this be summer–

Afraid that any light she turned on would reverberate through the small house, she moved through darkness, holding on to the door of her room, then the wall of the narrow hallway, then the wall by the stairs. The wall was cold, colder even then the air: it was as if that part of the house, the inner core of the stairwell, never really acknowledged seasons, was stuck in a changeless grey cold.

She got to the bathroom, had to fidget with the door a minute or two, the towels and robes on the back tangling with its close. Turned on the light and collapsed hurriedly onto the toilet. The googly eyes of the pink knitted dog on the bureau that held towels leered at her. She looked away. On her other side was a small closet, the sliding door open. Bits of her grandmother's dresses peeked out. They all seemed to be dark with little flowers. Oh but there were the lavender ones, the pale lilac that her grandmother liked for dress.

As she came out of the bathroom, she saw a light on in the kitchen. She didn't know how she hadn't seen it coming down. It must be her dad, she thought, sneaking some of his cheese.

Thinking she'd surprise him, she tiptoed towards the door, only realizing where the carpet sloped to linoleum, that it was Duke. He looked up from his cup of coffee, his cup of coffee with milk. Even in the dim light she could see that much, his cigar stub in the Mexican hat ash tray, his eyes bluer than ever in the fluorescent dim of the stove light, a pure grey blue like a cat in a story book, or maybe more like the yarn, the ball of yarn the cat pounces upon.

He saw her, leaned his head into his hands again, rubbed his hair.

Fear crawled between her legs, laddered her spine. Her mind raced for a hiding place, some place she could get to without embarrassment.

He wore an old fashioned T-shirt, the kind without sleeves, and boxer shorts. He looked so old in the dim fluorescent light, his hair greasy, the color of parakeet, his scalp yellow too, his skin thick and sagging and every part of it—below his eyes, cheeks and even his arms and chest yellowed. His bare skin, the parts she wasn't used to, seemed so thin, worn, the muscles seeming to be covered by an old sheathe of nylon, rumpled from having been tossed around.

She couldn't see the split in his boxer shorts, but she knew it was there, that boxer shorts had such things. Where could she go without his seeing her?

"Hey sugar," he said.

It was freezing in the kitchen, the wooden door open, the night air blowing in across miles of northern flatlands.

Shut the door someone, shut the windows.

"Hey doll, come here," he said. He motioned with one finger, then crooked it around the handle of his coffee cup

She didn't move.

"Aw, come on," he said. "I'm not going to eat you."

She wanted to run to her mother's bed. She wanted to run out of the door. Even the night would be better, even the dark.

"Okay, so don't come here," he said.

She realized that it wasn't coffee he was drinking, but something clearer and the smell, yeah, some kind of alcohol.

"What are you doing up here anyway, shit, this time of night? If you're going to go to bed, go to bed. If you're going to stay up and bother me, get your ass over here.

"I mean that's what you want isn't it, staring at me all day, following me around. Give me a break. And now you're not in the mood."

Her face burned. She looked at the floor. The lamp he'd lit cast a swell of light. He sat on the edge of it, she completely out.

Trying to remember his other voice "best girl," "doll," trying to come up with his wink, she stepped over to the table, but still beyond easy reach.

He shook his head abruptly as if he'd just dunked it into water, and put his bare arms around himself, rubbing his upper arms with his hands.

"Hey kid, don't worry about it," he said, his voice apologetic. "I don't want to give you a hard time."

"That's okay."

He got up and, with his arms still around himself, stomped over to the refrigerator. His boxer shorts curled around his buttocks. He never wore real shorts so it was strange to see his legs. They looked thick and knobby, grey blue when he opened up the fridge.

He pushed things around.

"You want a sandwich, doll?" He took out some milk, a cellophane bag of bologna, bread, butter.

Then he focused on the cake that had been put on top of the fridge. "Oh yeah. You want some of that cake? I think there's still some left—it was pretty darn good."

"No," she said. "I'm not hungry."

He took the stuff back to the table and began making himself a bologna sandwich. He seemed to take no notice of her now.

She did not want to run away anymore. She wanted to just sit down at the table, watch him make a sandwich, maybe eat some.

"You want something to drink? Say, how about some moo?" He laughed.

She tried to smile. "Nah."

"Come on, Les, have something" he insisted. "Now, you're up."

"I'll just get some water."

Striving for quiet, she slipped out of the chair rather than pushing it, walking delicately across the curling linoleum, but the faucet came on with a loud clang that unnerved her, the water rushed out in a small explosion. In her surprise, she filled the glass too full, spilling it down the front of her night dress, soaking that part through.

It took her a moment to understand what had happened, that she had spilled the water, that that was the cold shock over her chest, the spreading damp. As she did understand, she began to cry. She didn't want to cry; why was she always crying? She grabbed the stiff dishrag and began wiping at the chest of her nightdress.

Duke put down his bologna sandwich.

"Jesus," he muttered, bending over his plate, "give me a break." He combed his hair back, his fingers like claws through greasy feathers, again and again and again.

He brought his face up at last and scooted his chair out slightly, made as if he were about to get out of it, but didn't, opening his lap to her.

"Come on Les," he whispered, putting his arm out for her, "don't cry.

"Come on," he went on. "Be a big girl now, okay?"

She tried to stop, tried to smooth out her face, there must be something she could get right.

"Hey what's going on you two? Sneaking around the ice box huh?"

Les jumped, almost starting out loud.

It was her grandmother, her lips pressed together like a duck's bill into a toothless smirk.

"Hey, I woke up, thought what's that? One of those cows broke through the fence?" she laughed. "Felt almost like I was back on the farm." She grinned. "Aint used to so many folks sleeping under this old roof."

"Ooh Grandma is there a storm out?" Duke joked, "you look like you got blowed in a hurricane."

Even Les had to laugh. Her grandmother wore a net scarf that was still tied around her neck but all askew up top, her white hair pouring out around it.

"What I wonder is what you two found to eat," she said, pursing her toothless mouth into a sly smirk. "Anything good?"

* * *

It was cool, dark in the room, one arc of light coming through the window like a flying buttress, a mourning dove nearby.

She'd taken a nap. She'd meant to read–her grandma had a row of old Reader's igests in that attic-y bedroom and she had meant to read one after another, *Laughter is the Best Medicine, Humor in Uniform,* all the little jokes, the quotable quotes. But she'd fallen asleep. She could hear them all downstairs now, watching TV, banging in the kitchen.

She tried to slip back into her nap. She tried to remember something. First things. A sweater being put on, the pale pudge of her toddler arm. A porch with a swinging seat. Blackie, the dog they'd had when she was small, with a big sore on his side once; a train in early morning, climbing stairs through steam and fog.

And too, JFK being shot. She had been in first grade, which is pretty old for an first memory, but that one had been so big it seemed almost to crush everything before it. The principal had made the announcement over the loudspeaker. The loudspeaker was for buses, lunches, calling your teacher down to the office, and there she was talking about the President, killed, Dallas.

They had a special recess after the announcement and went outside into a sunny November afternoon, warmer than it should have been. The big girls, the ones from the sixth grade, lined up arm in arm in long scraggly rows like sideways trains, crying as they walked. All the other kids looked aimless, knowing they weren't supposed to be playing but not knowing what else to do out on the blacktop.

She went downstairs slowly.

They were watching Chicago, the Democratic convention.

They had driven through Chicago on the way. All highways and big green signs, her dad cursing the turn-offs.

It seemed like there was going to be some kind of problem. At least that's what the TV people said. Of course, they always said things like that, grim deep voices animated pulled-down mouths.

"What I don't understand is why all the protestors fixate on the poor Democrats?" her mom moaned. "They're the only ones that are going to work for peace at all. You just know it. Poor Humphrey."

"It's Johnson," Arne said.

Whenever Les pictured LBJ, she pictured a loose-faced hound dog. Partly because of his wrinkles and big sticking-out ears, and partly because she'd seen a picture in a magazine of him holding one of his beagles up by the ears. That seemed so mean, even though you could tell he really loved the beagle, that being mean was part of his way of loving it.

"Serves 'em right," Duke said. "Let all those stupid protestors screw around with them. The jerks."

"Duke," Ingrid said.

"Look, you've got a war, you've got to fight it," Duke said. "That's what you people just don't seem to understand; you can't just let it dribble out like molasses. And if those stupid longhairs don't like it, well then, they should just go to Sweden or something. Yep, just get out of here."

"Sounds like a good idea to me," Arne said. "Just get the hell out."

It was very small in her grandmother's living room, the couch wedged next to chairs, across from the TV. On the walls were mounted plates and photographs, a Swedish calendar, a portrait of her grandparents. Her grandmother had a young seamless face in the painting, but completely grey hair. Her grandfather had a boyish face, with a shock of reddish blonde bang that bisected the middle of his forehead.

Her grandma, who was sitting in a chair opposite the portrait, gestured towards it with one foot, trim in its black oxford.

"I always hated that picture," she said, smiling at Les. "Stephan looks just like my son, don't he? And I look like I never did have brown hair."

Les smiled back at her. "You look pretty though, Grandma."

"Hah! You go to Sweden, you better not expect to see my face again," Duke said.

"Sweden!" her grandma cried. "Who's going to Sweden? You know, they still write to me from over there every once in a while. Christmas cards."

"Christ, what they teach you boys these days I just don't know," Duke said, shaking his head.

"Oh come on," her dad said, pulling his nose. "Arne's not going to go to Sweden. He's just saying that. You know how boys are."

"Frankly, I don't think they'd take him anyway, with that asthma," her mom said. "At least I hope not."

Les could see Arne's face pale, the rough places in his skin looking like they were plastered on.

"You think he'll be 4F," Duke guffawed. "Naw. A big old boy like him."

Her grandma reached over and tousled Arne's hair. "I ought to tie a brick on you," she chuckled.

Arne pulled away sharply, as if hardly conscious of who had touched him. He stood up.

"I think that if Arne wants to go to Sweden, he should just go," Les said. "It's his life."

"You want him to end up in front of a firing squad?" Duke cried.

She swallowed. "He should do what he thinks is right. Honestly, you should, Arne."

"Give me a break," Arne said, stomping out to the kitchen.

"You folks should just leave that boy alone," Grandma said, also getting up. "After all, he's supposed to be on vacation."

"Oh-oh. What's happening now?" her mom said, leaning over to turn up the volume.

Les followed Arne out to the kitchen, trying to convey through a certain kind of smile that he really should just go to Sweden if he wanted.

But he didn't look at her. Her grandma re-centered the bruise cake on the table—"hey, Arne, want a piece of that good cake:" and turned to get some serving plates.

Les noticed the Mexican sombrero ash tray sitting in the dish rack and felt her face burn. She got up, went to the toaster, the window.

There was a metal bucket just below it. Dangling over its sides were the heads of two chickens. The heads hung like yoyos, wilted flowers, exploded puppets. Her stomach turned.

"I thought I'd make your dad some chicken and dumplings," her grandma said. "He'll like that, don't you think?"

"I guess so," Les said, rubbing her arms.

She looked to see if Arne had noticed the chickens; he was reading the paper now.

"Who killed them?"

"The guilty party's right here," Grandma said with a smile. "I always hate it, but when I got those old chickens I swore to myself I wasn't going to be soft-hearted. They're kind of stinky old things anyhow."

"Oh," Les said.

She went out to the porch. The chickens–the live chickens–stank, it was true. She had deliberately stayed away from that part of the yard after the first fun of looking through the wire at their shiny bright eyes, compulsive pecking.

"Oh my God, oh my God," her mother cried, her voice so urgent that Les immediately clambered back into the house, into the living room.

"Holy shit!" Arne said, who had beat her through the door.

"Arne!" said her father.

"Jesus Mary mother of God," Duke whispered.

"How can they be such idiots? What in the world?" her mother said.

"What's going on now?" said Grandma, who had stayed in the kitchen, dipping a finger into the dumpling batter.

The people on the screen streamed with blood. It streaked purple in places, over their foreheads, from their noses, down their shirt fronts and back; it glared where the lights shone.

That purple, those reds, were different from the neon edge along the side of the screen. That was just the way the reception was out here, her dad said. It streaked and pooled as people screamed, shouted.

Big sticks flailed incomprehensibly, policeman pivoted their tight-stretched hips, motorcycle jodhpurs, clustered their helmets over whatever, whomever, they beat, hiding them, so that only bits of leg, sleeve, sideburn, skin–the skin was always the shiniest part–that and the eyes–flashed.

Those dragged away, their bodies arched sags of resistance, were surrounded by other arms, screams of "pig". "Peace" flapped, gaped, on torn signs; "Out of Nam Now," crumpled.

Her mother had turned to stone.

Arne kept saying, "shit, shit, shit." Then, "that Daly's a pig if ever I saw one."

"That's showing them," Duke said.

"Arne," her father said.

Someone was being hit and hit again. Hands and shoulders blocked the camera, but angles of stick bypassed obstructions.

"Oh my God," her mother said. "What in the world?"

"My," Grandma said, now in the living room. "That ain't the police, is it?"

"They're going nuts," Duke said, shaking his head, half-smiling.
"Poor Humphrey," her mother said.

* * *

It was hard to sleep that night. The blinds upstairs jangled as the wind blew across the flat fields, the net curtains waved and flagged.

How could the police do those things? Police were supposed to be good.

She closed her eyes against the pictures. They used a light blue background for the body counts, though these days they showed a lot of footage of soldiers too, camouflaged legs running through weedy mire, the ramming echo of helicopter blades, urgent mutters of 'charlie'. Straw triangular hats too, beautiful triangular faces, square black pants running scared.

When she was little, they used to play the Star Spangled Banner at movie theaters, just before the show. The flag rippled upon the screen, and everyone would stand up, the bottoms of their seats flapping.

Her dad would put his hand over his heart. She didn't feel like she could do that, a girl child, who had never been, would never be, a soldier. Still, her heart rippled, furling and unfurling like the flag itself. Sometimes she sang along too, under her breath.

She had felt so proud. That she stood next to her dad, who'd been a soldier once, and that their country was the best country in all the world, the country that always wanted to help everyone, a country that was almost too good to be a country.

She woke to shouting.

She crept, trembling, into the stairwell, blue in the morning light. It was Duke and her mother. She waited for Arne's voice too. It would all come out now. There'd be crying next, even her dad. She felt sick.

But what she heard was her mother saying 'tiles', 'closet', 'all that junk', and Duke groaning, 'oh come on Ing. I did too finish that closet.'

'leave like that...'

'give me a break.'

'timing couldn't be worse… the job wasn't so great either…'

'Jesus Christ, woman.'

'should have done it myself.…knew that…"

Screen door slamming.

She tiptoed down. Anger still jangled the kitchen; Les could feel the screen door reverberating with Duke's slam, the brusque rev of his car.

"You just got to be nice to him, that's all," her grandmother said.

"Momma, I am nice to him," Ingrid said. "My goodness. I let him stay in my house for weeks, didn't I? But am I supposed to just let him walk out on a job, a job I was paying him for?"

Grandma sighed, "oh Ing."

"And then I come out here on my vacation and break my back trying to get things fixed up a little and he waltzes in and he hasn't even been working and he can't lift a gosh darn finger but just waits there like a king for you to dish him out some grub. Doesn't say a damn word about the cupboards; doesn't do a damn thing except to get his greasy fingerprints on one when he deigns to get his own coffee cup because we're not fast enough." She began wiping one of the newly painted cupboards with the dishrag. "And I don't even say a thing."

"Why do you have to get started up on all this darn old stuff anyhow?"

"Mom, you know I like helping you a little when I come out. Anyway, I don't do much."

"Sure, you do. You just said you broke your back. I don't invite people to my house to break their backs."

"Oh Mom." Ingrid paused, scowled, wiped at the cupboard again. "Don't take one thing I said–"

"Poor old Duke–he just don't see things the way you do. He's not interested in fixing up houses. House don't make a dadburned bit of difference to him."

"You can't tell me he doesn't like things nice. He's always talking about this great hotel here, that beautiful resort over there. He seems to like them plenty."

"Well, sure," the old lady chuckled. "Nice is okay with him if it's delivered on a silver platter. But he don't care much if <u>he's</u> the one who's gotta do it."

A rash of anger rose up Ingrid's neck. "It's just not fair. To take and take, and then expect us to bail him out all the time."

"Oh sweetie, he could do more, sure. But he does do things. Keeps me company every once in a while, drives me here and there. Maybe he does expect me to cook for him, wash his clothes sometimes. But it's kind of nice to have someone to cook for, do for. Especially when you can't hardly see straight."

"Mom—"

"I'm not saying that makes him right, mind you. But it's just the way he is, Ing. You know that. He was funny as a little boy and then the army made him worse, a lot worse, and now with all that golf, and card games too. You just gotta feel sorry for someone like that. He's just never had things right, not ever; never been right neither."

Les listened quietly as her mother pulled out the broom, began sweeping the kitchen.

So, he was gone again. She tried to ignore the relief that flooded through her. She tried to feel sorry, like her grandmother said. Even felt sorry.

* * *

They walked to town to pick up the mail.

She wished Arne hadn't come.

"Shit," he said.

There was cover if she kept her face down. Her white sneakers were tearing at the toe. There was a line along the rim dividing the softly worn part of the sole from the part that still held a tread.

"Come on, Les, look, what if he comes back, the jerk?" Arne said.

"He won't come back."

She slowed down, kicking a small stone as she walked.

"How do you know? Shit. You didn't expect him to come this time either."

It was a rough stone with a granulated surface. Like coal, but not so dark and shiny.

"I know you didn't."

She kicked it only a little each time, moderating her gait so it seemed as if she was just walking. She had to concentrate to do that, to not add extra force to the kicking leg.

"It's okay here, Grandma's house is so little. But our house is different. It's a completely different story."

One big kick, one big but quiet kick? No.

Kick, kick, shuffle kick. Just like walking, like nothing was happening at all.

"Do you hear me?" he said.

She stopped. She looked up to him. His eyes were shaped like their mom's, she thought. She'd never noticed that.

"So what?" she said. "So what if he comes to our house? He isn't going to kill anybody."

"What a jerk," he said. "Do you know what a goddamn jerk you are?"

She walked faster, very fast. He grabbed her arm. She pulled away. A farmer, hunkered down in a big white car, approached slowly, his face red even through the blue glare of the windshield.

Arne loosened his hold. The farmer peeked suspiciously over the steering wheel, but drove by.

She walked away from Arne, her tennis shoes flattening into the stride.

"I'm going to tell," he shouted.

She started to run.

"I swear it Les if you don't tell I will," he shouted.

She felt like she was running very fast. She wasn't going to look back at him. Looking back was where you lost speed.

But she heard him catching up.

She tried to raise each leg higher, to not even come down upon the toe. She thought of the way her swimming coach told them to swim, stretching arms long above the surface of the water, then diving them down like spears. She thought about the feeling she had after they'd been swimming in sweatclothes and sneakers and they stripped down to their bathing suits and their bodies slid through the water like otters.

She ran for three long blocks. She was surprised she could keep ahead, Arne's legs so much longer than hers, boy legs. She tried not to think about that, to just keep going. Then she reached the main street of town, Route 218.

It was only two lanes, but a highway. Cars went 75 just outside of town and sometimes right through it. Car coming now, looking familiar in the way of any big roar car, but she was running really fast now, didn't think of the car except as savior, that if she could just beat it, get across to the corn lot, railroad tracks, that car would slow down Arne, head him off, Arne would have to wait for that car, and wait for a while. These drivers would slow down lots if they almost hit a kid.

She took one step off the curb, sure she could beat the car just as Arne grabbed her. She realized in that instant that it was Duke's car, that it was Duke driving that car, and that she had better not cross it.

The car squealed to a stop, twisting towards the curb.

"Are you crazy? You idiot!" Arne squeezed her arm so it hurt. His face was bright red and he was breathing heavily. Then he let go. Bending at the waist, he put his hands on his sides and coughed. It was a choking cough. Coughed again, gagging as if he were vomiting.

The noise wrenched her throat, stomach. Goddammit, why'd he have to run so hard anyway, this air so bad for him. She touched his back, hoping he wouldn't sense her hand.

"What in the hell are you kids doing? Don't you know better than to dart around like that next to a highway? Jesus Christ. People'd think you were one of these bumpkins, never seen a highway, goddammit."

Duke, out of his car now, poked the air with his cigar.

Les pretended not to hear him, kept her eyes on Arne, still doubled over. Took her hand from his back though; didn't want to touch anyone with Duke around.

Duke, putting his cigar back in his mouth, substituted concern for some of the anger. "Jesus Christ" he muttered, forehead wrinkling;

bent down next to Arne, the cigar up by Arne's face. Idiot, Les thought. Arne turned away sure enough, still coughing.

"Come on boy, you okay? Whoosh."

"It's all this pollen," Les said.

"Pollen, shit," Arne said, pulling himself straight enough to give her a look of contempt. Then cleared his throat with a hawking spit to the ground.

Keys jingling, Duke stepped back to the car door.

"Come on, Arne. Let me take you back to Grandma's, huh? You got some of that breathing medicine back there, don't ya?"

Arne, whose breath still wheezed, didn't look at Duke, but turned and began walking back the way they had just run.

"Come on Arne," Duke tried again. "It can't be good to stay out here after all that. Let's get home to your folks."

Arne didn't answer him, kept on walking, a nonchalant walk that didn't go with the red blotches on his neck, his purpling ears.

Duke squinted down at her. "How about you, Les?" He opened the door. "Come on, doll. We'll get there quick."

She felt Arne waiting for her. Stopping, turning.

She pivoted, ran the short light steps to her brother, took his hand. Trembling, "you better just go," she said to Duke.

"Les–"

"You better just go now, okay?"

She tried to keep her face straight, to not let Duke draw her into any kind of play-acting. It was very hard. Her face seemed to tug itself towards smiles, towards apologies, her face drawn like a magnet to the pole of nice. Her stern expression was also an act; she couldn't even tell what expression was truly hers, would be hers, if she could manage it, only that her brother stood next to her, breathing jaggedly, and that she owed him something, something not nice.

"You better just leave us alone."

They took no short cuts home. Les tried to count Arne's breaths rather than steps, trying through her silent count to sooth them, order them, as they re-ordered themselves, into something regulated, calm. Trying through her count not to think.

They still held hands, walking. It felt strange, yet also required. She had never held hands with him before, and felt a kind of current running through their fingertips. It ran through her arms and down her legs; it seemed to start both in her core and in his, to come from him, even as it came from her, as if she were plugged in to an outlet and running on battery at once.

Everything was still in comparison to that flow. The overhanging branches, the canopy of leaves, the white clapboard houses to the sides. The stillness like an envelope around a letter, a theatre around an ovation, an inhalation before a roar.

Then she seemed to feel it running through the stillness too. She could feel it—their flow–in the brilliance of the leaves, the gleam of house paint, the sparkle of mica in the pavement, even in the opacity of mail box posts and telephone poles, the iron insignias on doors, the muted screens of open windows.

She wanted to reach out to the brilliance, but she seemed to lose track of it every time she tried to take hold. It was like her count of her brother's breath. She seemed to find it and lose it and find it and lose it, never getting close to a total.

The current was so strong, so big, that for a long while she didn't really mind its slipperiness. But as they got nearer to her grandmother's house, the losing part, the searching and forgetting, the stopping to look for the thread, seemed to take over, and the finding only to be glimpsed, and soon she was conscious that their stride was just an imitation of the strong walk with which they had begun; and, on her part at least, an affectation. They dropped hands.

There they were. The black rickety shed on one side (the stall where her grandma had once kept a young bull named Popeye and where the chickens now bowed and scraped). The garden on the other, its daisy-shaped windflowers starkly plastic, its blue hydrangeas hugely frowsy, its good black dirt grayed and powdery, the leaves of the rows of sweet corn peeling halfway from the stalk like a woman too tired to fully undress.

The plastic daisies twirled slowly. She could see what must be a breeze in the kale leaves too, the edge of billow in their dark curls. But she felt no hint of it inside herself. It was as if the current had gone underground now, and everything it had supported sunk heavily onto her shoulders.

"You okay, Arne?"

He grunted.

He walked ahead of her now, his calves brown above big sneakers, that part of him healthy enough. He was straining his head to look for something. What? Oh, Duke's car probably. No, it wasn't back, was it?

No. No, it wouldn't be.

Busy at the house. Her grandma was pumping water into a big tin watering can. The water came out in great splashes that splattered against the can with intermittent bangs. Her mother was standing to the side, inspecting the pump's paint, running a finger up and down the peeled spots. Even her father was on the porch, reading a paperback, his black leather Army-issued shoes stretched into the sunlight.

Her grandma wore one of her dark flowered dresses with a brighter flowered apron on top. Around the pump were flashes of zinnias, beautiful purple ones, orange and red. They seemed to shine in the sun, the flowers on her grandma's dress too.

As Les watched, she realized that the pump shone too, despite its peeling paint. That the splashing spurting water sparkled. That even her mom, who wore an old white shirt and shorts, seemed to hold sunlight in her squint, clean and bright and present.

Her dad looked up a moment from his book and waved, smiling. The sun caught the edge of his teeth, the crook of grin.

She waved back.

"Hey," Grandma said. "You get me any letters?"

"Oh no, we forgot," Les said. "We forgot to even check."

"You forgot the mail?"

"I'm sorry, yeah. We just forgot," Les said. She shrugged.

Arne snorted.

"Probably just bills anyway," Grandma sighed. "They don't go anywhere."

With a sheepish smile, Arne walked past his grandmother who tried to reach up to tousle his hair. He stooped slightly so she could get it.

But Les walked over to her grandmother, her mother, her dad.

Maybe she'd bake another cake, she thought.

Or maybe, she thought, her mother would let her paint the pump.

And if she wouldn't, well, then maybe she would just insist on it.

And if her mom still didn't want to let her, well, then maybe she'd just take the brush and do it anyway.

Maybe.

Les
Suburban Maryland
Election Day, November 1968

She worked all day. It was windy, grey. She stood outside her old school, just below the little mosaic of football players, ballerinas. You had to be very careful to stand so many feet from the big double doors. That, she had learned, was one of the main rules about election day. You couldn't talk to people right by the doors.

Her jaw ached from smiling so much. It was probably stupid to think that just by smiling, she could convince someone on those last steps to the polling booth, that something had to be done about the war.

But smiling was all she knew, smiling when she didn't really feel like it, and now it was down to the wire. People were fighting, dying, Americans, Vietnamese. Didn't Vietnamese count?

Men were the nicest to her, men with slightly grizzled whiskers. Young men too with blue work pants, tan boots. She seemed to know how to smile in just the right way to get them to stop, listen. She could feel in her cheeks when she'd gotten it. Even if they nodded their heads sorrowfully, meaning they were going to have to vote for Nixon anyway, or Wallace (her junior high had gone for him in their mock vote), they still would stop, and she could almost make herself believe, she could at least make herself hope, that in those next few seconds they might rethink things, that even as they shook their heads, their hearts might shift.

Black men too would listen, but they were usually already on her side.

Women, especially a certain crisply-teased, straight-mouthed sort of white woman, walked brusquely past her, acted as if she was worse than an interruption, kept their distance as if she were a disease.

Her flagpole was just across the driveway. Though it wasn't her flag-pole anymore. The flagpole that she and Bruce Beebee had manned the year before. Someone had hung up the flag. She looked at it some-times when there was a gap in the voters.

It jutted and swelled in the wind, then clumped against the flagpole in a sideway's heap. Still, that was ordinary enough. No one would be able to tell that it had been dropped, she thought. Which seemed kind of strange to her. For all the fuss they made about burning, burying, about never ever letting it touch the ground, you would have thought that there'd be some sign that it wasn't the same anymore, that it could never be the same.

But there wasn't really. From the outside, you wouldn't have been able to tell.

Afterword

Writers often use the palette of their lives to color their characters; trying for realism, one looks to the real one knows. This use of real life details may make one's characters look like real people.

In the case of this book, none of the characters is a real person; no character is a portrait or even a reflection of a real person; any resemblance is purely coincidental. The views voiced by characters are the views of the characters only and not my own.

Additionally, I want to stress that none of the events in this book actually happened, other than those events—RFK's assassination, the Chicago convention–that are clearly historical. The book is fiction, not memoir. What is real is the time; what is made up—everything that happens to these characters in that time.

Acknowledgements

Many thanks to the readers of my blog, http://Manicddaily.wordpress.com, for their generous encouragement of my work, with special gratitude to Joy Anne Jones (an online poet posting as Hedgewitch) for her invaluable counsel. Thanks too to Brian Miller and Claudia Schoenfeld who introduced me to the world of online poetry and to my old writing-in-notebooks buddy, Jeannie Hutchins.

More than thanks to my brother, Robert Gustafson, for his unfailing love and support, to Meredith Martin, Christina Martin, and Heron Haas for their sweetness, creativity and indulgence (of both my writing and non-writing foibles), and, finally, to my dearest Jason Martin, whose keen editorial eye and loving spirit made publication possible.

BackStroke Books

www.ingramcontent.com/pod-product-compliance
Lightning Source LLC
Chambersburg PA
CBHW031337170626
46807CB00002B/746